STARS AND WANDERERS

Edited by Ellen Parry Lewis

Metal Lunchbox Publishing

Cover design by: SF Varney
Twitter @sfvarney

THE TELESCOPE

By Virginia Parrish

The summer that Frank DiGiovanni got the telescope, he was fourteen, his brother Del was thirteen, and his sister Lennie and I were twelve.

It was like every other summer before air conditioning and community pools. Our backyard and the DiGiovannis' backyard ran together, giving us a double play area unlimited by fences or landscaping. We didn't have much of a lawn in the back because of the constant scuffling of kids and dogs. Nobody bothered to water or fertilize backyards in our neighborhood anyway. Sometimes Frank's and Del's friends would come over and play baseball on an improvised diamond. Frank, who was always in charge of everything, drew the bases in the dust. This led to countless, sometimes physical, disputes about who was safe and who was out. Lennie and I watched from the sidelines. Girls didn't play baseball.

On most afternoons, we would sit on top of the picnic table because the grass and dust made us itch, and watch the heat rising from the concrete back steps. When Lennie and I were little, we had sometimes pretended we were explorers lost in the desert, and had staggered panting around the yard until Frank and Del had told us to stop being stupid and get some Kool-Aid. Mrs. DiGiovanni always left us a gallon of Kool-Aid in the refrigerator, and it was always gone by the end of the day. Mrs. DiGiovanni supplied our cookies, too. At the time, I was envious of Frank, Del, and Lennie, but now I think she did it out of guilt.

She worked. She was the only mother in the neighborhood who had a job, and everyone thought it was pretty peculiar, especially since Mr. DiGiovanni's news agency seemed to be prosperous, and it didn't look like she *had* to work. She wasn't one of those creative types who worked for self-expression, either. Eight hours a day, she sat in a sewing factory, stitching collars onto ladies' dresses. I'd heard my parents call the DiGiovannis money-hungry, and my father had made some pretty severe remarks about the kids being neglected, but the kids seemed all right to me, and I loved the Kool-Aid. In fact, I wished my mother worked. Lennie had three Betsy McCall dolls to my one, which made me jealous even though we didn't play with them anymore, and she always had money for a comic book and a chocolate Coke when we went downtown.

Lennie and I were really into comic books that summer. I was an avid fan of Wonder Woman and Supergirl, and I eagerly awaited each new issue. I thought it grossly unfair that boys had Superman, Batman, the Flash, Green Arrow, and countless other heroes, while we girls had only Wonder Woman and Supergirl —and to tell the truth, Supergirl was pretty dumb. I said, "Hera help me!" and "Suffering Sappho!" a lot that July and even tried to learn to use a lasso till Frank started calling me Annie Oakley.

My family always had dinner in the basement during the summer because by the time my mother was done cooking, the kitchen would be so hot it was unbearable. We'd eat at an old table near the washing machine and enjoy the damp coolness. After we finished eating, we had to carry all the dirty dishes up the stairs, and I'd have my regular fight with my little brother Ricky over whose turn it was to do the dishes. I figured Ricky should do them every night because I was old enough to go outside after dark, and he had to stay inside anyway. Sometimes I could intimidate him into doing my work, but if I threatened him too much, he'd cry, and my mother would be all over me. I told Lennie that Frank and Del were pains, all right, but I'd trade Ricky for them any day.

After dinner, in the twilight and then in the dark, we'd play kitty-can. My mother called it kick-the-can, but that was something only old people said, and we thought it was stupid. Sometimes we'd let the Cooney kids from down the block play, but mostly it was just the four of us, night after night, playing a variation of hide-and-seek.

"Kitty-can on Del!"

"Kitty-can on Janice!"

That summer, Frank was conscious of the fact that he'd be starting high school in September, and he bossed us around more than ever. Sometimes when we were playing, he'd complain that kitty-can was a baby game, and he'd play badly on purpose. I hated that because kitty-can had always been the most fun thing we did, and I still loved it. Del and I were pretty good hiders and runners. In fact, we were the best. Lennie liked playing it as much as I did, but she always picked the same hiding places, and she wasn't much of a runner. Del and I would conspire and keep the other two going.

"Hide in the Venturas' hedge," he'd tell me, "and when Frank goes your way, make a little noise. Then I'll run in and kick the can."

I would do as he said, and it would always work. Del and I hardly ever had to be It. We'd play until my mother yelled from the back door.

"Janice! Time to come in!"

That would break up the game because the three of them wouldn't play without me. They'd go in then too, even though nobody called them. I used to wonder if Mrs. DiGiovanni would let them stay out all night.

One day early in August, Lennie and I were sitting on the picnic table, drinking Kool-Aid and reading new comic books. I had been astounded to read the cover blurb on one: *Superman Marries Lois Lane.* I had eagerly handed over my dime, but now I threw the comic book down in disgust.

"What's the matter?" Lennie asked.

"I think it's really rotten the way they get you to buy a comic book and it turns out to be a lie."

"Didn't he marry her?"

"Yeah, but it was really Clark Kent because he had amnesia because of Kryptonite, and then when he remembered, he had to travel back in time and change it all. So he really didn't."

"Well, he did sort of marry her. It's not really a *lie*."

"It is too."

"It is not. They couldn't put a lie right on the cover of a comic book like that."

"Sure they could. Why couldn't they?"

"Cause it's a sin."

"That's really dumb, Lennie."

"It is not!" Lennie sat up straight and put down her new Green Arrow. "They just can't put a lie out in public like that because it's against the law to put a sin on the cover of a comic book."

"How do you know?" Sometimes Lennie really drove me crazy with this sin business. As a minority Public in a town where all kids identified themselves as either Catholic or Public, I knew Lennie could talk circles around me about sin. I usually tried to shut her up. This day, I was out of luck. She was gathering breath to come back at me when Frank and Del walked out the back door.

"Frank!" Lennie yelled.

"What?"

"Isn't it against the law to put a sin on the cover of a comic book?"

I rolled my eyes at Del.

"God, Lennie, you ask the dumbest questions," Frank said in exasperation.

"Well, is it or isn't it?"

"What are you talking about?"

Lennie reviewed our discussion in detail while Del snickered. Frank didn't laugh, though. He liked it when he was called on to settle an argument. It made him feel like a big shot. We would fight with Del about practically anything, but none of us would contradict Frank. After due consideration, he said, "Well, I don't think it's exactly a lie, so I guess it isn't a sin."

"See?" Lennie asked me triumphantly.

"Shut up, Lennie! You're the one who went on about all that sin and stuff. I just said it was a lie, that's all."

"Well, if it was a lie, it would be a sin, wouldn't it?"

"I guess so. I don't know all that much about sin, anyway." Not only was I a Public, I was a non-practicing Public. We didn't go to church.

"That's because you're not Catholic," Lennie said kindly.

"I *know*."

"Well, Frank said it wasn't a sin."

"Good for Frank," I muttered. It was as close as I would get to disrespect. "Anyway, I still think it's rotten to trick people into buying the comic book that way."

Del had picked up my discarded Superman. "Trade you for the new Aquaman," he offered.

"Okay, but I'll tell you right now, they don't really get married."

"They do too," Lennie put in.

"All right, all right, but they don't stay married."

Del grinned and whispered something to Frank. They both laughed.

"What's so funny?" I asked.

"Nothing that little girls can hear," Del told me.

"You're a creep, Del DiGiovanni," I said angrily, "and you can keep your stupid Aquaman."

I jumped off the table and marched over to sit on the back step even though the concrete was broiling hot. Lennie was right behind me. Frank and Del shrugged and walked off.

"Del is a creep!" I said to Lennie.

"I know. I always tell you."

"Do you know what he said about me?"

Lennie stared at her bare feet. "I don't think he said anything about you."

"Then what was he whispering about?"

Lennie wiggled her toes and kept staring at them. "Superman and Lois Lane, I guess."

"Don't be stupid. How could Del have secrets about Superman and Lois Lane?"

"Cause they got married."

"Well, that's no secret. It was right in the comic book. What's the big deal?"

Lennie continued to contemplate her grimy feet. "Because, Janice, *you know.*"

"I know what?" I was getting really annoyed with her.

Lennie stopped looking at her feet and gazed at a bird gliding across the sky. "You know...when people get married..." She paused delicately.

I finally figured out what she meant. "You mean Del was saying that about Superman and Lois Lane? Ew, yuck, Lennie, that's disgusting!"

"Well, if they were married, it wouldn't be a sin."

"Lennie, I am so tired of hearing about sin, and I think your brother Del is a rotten, dirty, disgusting creep, and I am going to go in now, and don't you dare come knock on my door tonight because I probably won't even want to play kitty-can." I stomped into the house and slammed the screen door behind me. It was even hotter inside, and I felt the sweat running in little streams down my back and down my front too, and it made me shiver.

I went to my room, closed the door, and sat in my blue chair, gazing at my shelf full of Nancy Drew books. Nancy was almost as good as Wonder Woman and definitely better than Supergirl. She and Ned Nickerson never even kissed, which was fine with me. I thought Wonder Woman had the right idea. She didn't have a boyfriend.

I wondered exactly what Del had said. Did he say any bad words? In spite of myself, I kept thinking of Superman and Lois Lane like a crude picture I had seen drawn on the lavatory wall at school, and I started to cry. I sat there and sobbed and sniffled for about ten minutes before my mother heard me and came in. She never knocked.

"What's the matter?" she asked.

"Nothing."

"Well, there must be something the matter, or you wouldn't be crying."

"I sort of had a fight with Lennie."

"What about?"

"Nothing."

My mother looked affronted. She always did when I wouldn't tell her things. "Okay, if you don't want to talk about it," she said in a martyred tone. "It'll probably blow over, and you and Lennie will be friends again tomorrow. Now go blow your nose and wash your face."

I did, although I thought it was pretty dumb to wash my face in the middle of the day, and then I went back into my room and read *The Bungalow Mystery* until dinnertime.

By the time we finished dinner, I'd gotten over my annoyance with Lennie, although I still didn't want anything to do with Del, and I went outside without anyone coming for me. Tim and Maureen Cooney were already there waiting to play kitty-can with us. That made me mad all over again because when Tim was there, Del partnered with him instead of me because he was a better runner than I was, and Maureen, who was only eleven and fat, whined that everybody cheated by not moving the can all the way back to base before we started counting. She was right, too, but we ignored her.

Perversely, although I hated Del, I wished Tim would go home so Del and I could play against Frank and Lennie. I was surprised, then, when I hid in the bushes at the back of the Daltons' garage, to find Del slipping in beside me.

"Lennie says you're mad at me," he whispered.

"Shut up."

"What are you mad for?"

"You're a creep."

"Thanks a lot."

"You're a disgusting creep."

"Takes one to know one."

"You make me sick."

"Kitty-can on Janice and Del in the bushes behind Daltons' garage," yelled fat little Maureen, and Del and I were condemned to go back to base and wait to be freed.

"You and your big mouth got us caught," Del complained.

"*My* big mouth? You started it!"

"I did not. You were mad first."

"Shut up."

"Come on, Jan, what are you mad about?"

I wouldn't answer. It would be pretty stupid to say, "I'm mad because you said something dirty about Superman and Lois Lane," and anyway, I wasn't even sure that was really it. Luckily, Frank ran in and freed us just then, the can clanking noisily across the yard, and fat little Maureen puffing after it. I didn't see Del anymore during that game, and my mother called me in soon afterward.

It was even hotter the next day, and the four of us were languishing on the picnic table again. Frank, Del, and Lennie were reading comic books, but I was continuing with *The Bungalow Mystery*. I had decided during the night that I wasn't going to read comic books for a while.

Del reached over and poked me in the ribs. I jumped and dribbled Kool-Aid down my leg.

"Delano DiGiovanni!" I yelled. "What are you trying to do?"

"Nancy Drew is really stupid," he said. "That's for fifth-graders."

"It is not," I disagreed, all the more heatedly because he was right. "Look, you made me get Kool-Aid on my shorts."

"So?"

"So my mother will have a fit. It's grape Kool-Aid, and these are tan shorts, and I'm going to tell her it's all your fault."

"Who cares?"

"Del, I don't know what's wrong with you, but will you please shut up and leave me alone?" I was starting to feel really funny about the way Del was acting. I sneaked a sideways look at him. He was reading Lennie's Green Arrow and frowning. His dark brown crewcut was damp from the heat, and for the first time, I noticed the fine dark hair on his upper lip. I realized with astonishment that Del was going to have to shave, maybe even soon.

I had been thinking a lot about shaving lately. There was fuzzy hair just starting under my arms. I knew I was supposed to shave it off, but I had no idea how to go about it, and I sure wasn't going to ask my mother. She'd say something sickening about her little girl growing up. I figured I'd wait till my parents were out sometime, and then I'd use my father's razor and hope I didn't cut myself and bleed all over everything.

Del caught me looking at him and grinned. The hair on his lip looked almost like a mustache. It was really weird. Here was Del, a teenager, with practically a mustache, and I hadn't noticed it happening.

"What are you looking at?" he asked.

"Not you, that's for sure," I sniffed.

"You going to tell me why you were mad yesterday?"

"Ask Lennie."

"Don't ask me!" Lennie protested.

"What was Janice mad about?" Del asked.

"I don't know," Lennie replied.

"Liar!"

"I am not!"

"You are too!"

Frank slammed his fist down on the table. "Shut up!" he yelled. "I'm tired of listening to you guys! I'm sick of your stupid fights and your stupid baby comic books!" That didn't make a whole lot of sense because he had just been reading Batman.

Del turned on him furiously. "You shut up, Frank! Who do you think you are, always telling everybody what to do? You think you're sick of us? Well, I'm sick of you! I'm sick of being your brother, and I'm sick of being bossed around!"

Lennie and I stared in open-mouthed astonishment. Del was really building up to a great climax when his voice cracked, and Lennie and I giggled. He turned to us with all the anger he had been aiming at Frank, but we kept giggling. His bottom lip started to tremble.

"You—you go to hell!" he screamed at us, and he ran into the house. Frank tore after him, yelling. Lennie and I just sat there on the picnic table, and after a while we picked up our Kool-Aid and drank it.

It was that night that the telescope came. None of us had known anything about it, not even Frank. The DiGiovannis bought their kids presents for no reason sometimes. I guess it was because they had all that extra money from Mrs. DiGiovanni working. This time the present was a telescope. It was a big white cylinder with brass knobs and fittings on it. Mr. DiGiovanni set it up and showed Frank how to use it and then went into the house. Frank knew all about astronomy from school. He was really smart, and he was going to be an Air Force test pilot someday, or maybe even an astronaut, so he needed to know where all the planets were. That made sense to me, just like if you were a truck driver, you needed to know where all the cities were.

Lennie and I jumped up and down impatiently for our turn to look, but Del just stood there with his hands in his pockets. Del and Frank hadn't said much to each other that evening, and I wondered how their argument had finished that afternoon. I'd asked Lennie, but she said that by the time she'd gone in, they had stopped screaming at each other, and she wasn't sure who had won.

"You can look now," Frank said to me. "I've got it focused on Saturn."

I got to go first because I wasn't his sister, so he was nicer to me than he was to Lennie. I looked through the telescope at Saturn, floating millions and millions of miles away from the four of us in the backyard, a place where there was no summer, no comic books, no games of kitty-can in the twilight.

It was the most beautiful thing I'd ever seen. The sky in space was black, blacker than anything on earth, as if I'd never really seen blackness before. Against it, the sphere of Saturn was a floating marble swirled with pink and brown and gold. The rings that went around it at a slant were shining white, and in the black, black sky beyond it were stars that glittered like Fourth-of-July sparklers.

I knew I was taking longer than my turn, but I couldn't tear myself away until Lennie shoved me.

"Come on, Jan, don't hog it," she said.

I didn't even answer, but I stepped back unwillingly. I wanted to look through that telescope forever and ever.

"Del," I whispered, "wait till you see it. It's fantastic. It's so different than seeing it in a book. It's like you could touch it."

Del didn't answer.

"Del," I said, exasperated, "what's the *matter* with you? Don't you want to see Saturn?"

"I don't care," he shrugged.

"Well, I think you're stupid if you don't look."

"You think I'm stupid anyway."

"What are you talking about?"

"How come you said I was a creep?"

"My God, Del, I must have called you a creep about a million times in my life, and it was never any big deal, and now you're acting like your feelings are all hurt or something."

"Well, don't you think my feelings are hurt?"

"I think you're crazy. If your feelings get hurt every time somebody calls you a name, you're going to be pretty miserable."

"That's right, I am."

By now our voices were raised, and Frank turned to us in annoyance. "Will you two shut up!" he snapped.

"Why?" Del asked sarcastically. "Do you have to listen to the planets or something?"

"Do you want a turn at this or not?" Frank asked, trying to show off how patient and generous he could be.

"No!" shouted Del. "You can keep your stupid planets and your stupid stars and everything else you think you know all about!"

And before any of us could stop him, he kicked the tripod of the telescope, and it fell with a crash, the lenses shattering on the dusty ground. Then he turned and ran past the Daltons' garage. Lennie took off for the house, screaming for her parents, and Frank went down on his knees, picking up pieces of the telescope and cursing in words I'd never heard anyone say. For a minute I stood there, and then I ran after Del. I knew where he would be.

"Del," I whispered, as I squeezed through the bushes against the back of the Daltons' garage. "Are you okay?"

I couldn't see him very well as he crouched there in the dark, but I knew he wiped his eyes with his hand. I sat down beside him.

"Yeah, I'm okay," he whispered back. "My dad's going to kill me for breaking the telescope, though."

"Well, my God, Del, it was a stupid thing to do! Why in the world..."

"Don't you start on me!" he interrupted, forgetting to whisper.

"Sh!" I cautioned. "They'll find us—and anyway, I'm not starting on you, I just don't know why you did it."

Del was silent for a moment, picking a small leaf off the bush in front of us and tearing it to pieces that he dropped on the dusty ground. "I'm sick of Frank," he muttered.

I tried to act like I understood, although I was sure I didn't. "We all get sick of Frank sometimes. He thinks he's such a big shot. Oh, but Del, I wish you hadn't done it. I wanted you to see Saturn. It was so beautiful."

I felt a lump come up in my throat just thinking that I could never see it again because Del had broken the telescope. Then I realized that Del would never see it at all, and that made me so sad that I couldn't say anything. Instead, I reached out and put my hand on his cheek, and he covered it with his. We sat there like that for a minute, and then we heard his father yelling, "Delano DiGiovanni, you get your tail over here! You've got a lot to answer for!"

I started to pull my hand away, but Del held onto it. He straightened his shoulders, and then, before I knew what he was doing, he leaned over and kissed me, right on the mouth. Just for a moment, I looked into his eyes, and in the moonlight, the tears in them were as bright as the rings of Saturn.

THE GREAT MARCELO'S MULTIVERSE SEANCE

By Andrew Bockhold

On reading days, Marcelo programmed a thunderstorm to roll across the bare concrete walls. The clouds and rain coursed along in three dimensions, which he controlled with the sweep of his arms like Moses on the banks of the Red Sea. And just as the seance to come, he moved the elements into a semblance of order. Marcelo even programmed a single butterfly to flit through the seeming chaos of each storm. He named it Anya after his dead wife. Always Anya, for this was the room he built to find her.

One of Marcelo's calculations indicated she would enjoy a hologram of a lake. A stream fed the pool near her house where she lived alone. For in this alternate universe she'd never met Marcelo. She *had* enjoyed the stream that ran beside their old home in their shared universe, where they lived together before the wars. These intersections pleased Marcelo. For in his universe, she'd been dead for fifteen years. Everything he calculated now was just possible Anyas.

He programmed several lightning strikes to announce the beginning of the seance. He found it opened up his clients to the experience. Fear and awe were still powerful motivators, he mused. He stood in the middle of the storm, a refuge or guide to the universes adjacent to our own.

"Please come into the warmth, I implore you, ladies and gentleman, please, please come, I have such delights to share with you!" The Great Marcelo beckoned. He needed his customers to be comfortable, willing to part with their identi-cache freely. And he wouldn't deny his enjoyment of the drama, the spectacle.

Tonight, he ushered a family into the reading room, and the soft velvet drapes parted to allow them entrance. Marcelo used real fabric for certain textures, no nano-holograms. Fingertips caressed the red drapes, and ripples of gasps would run through a group before sitting at the reading table. The power of human touch had fallen entirely out of fashion after the antibiotic collapse brought old diseases back. It was a retro treat for people to run their palms over the velvety folds. That is, palms lucky enough to be approved for non-essential goods and services.

Marcelo often ruminated on the consequences of the global currency collapse. Businesses now chose their patrons exclusively. Potential customers had to wait for company approval before attempting to acquire their products. And the system was lock-step, like the old blockchain markets. Even Marcelo himself had approval rights for his customers, but he was locked out of most other purchasing because his credit took two hits: bankruptcy and 'marketing deficit' feedback. To have him as a customer tarnished brands even if he could pay.

Marcelo created two popular configurations of the room. First, a classic den of velvet, plush chairs, and various shades of red. The room could be dimmed to the color of blood, thick with crimson. Candlelight reached weakly out the windows to the programmed countryside after dark. The second room was elegant, colder with sharp edges, muted blues, and a glossy sheen. The sterile features mimicked the cold equations that organized the natural worlds. Each had its charms, and each reflected the temperament of his handpicked participants.

The room's focal point was the community table around

which Marcelo's customers crowded to see the intense holograms. Marcelo had nothing as kitschy as a crystal ball. He wanted people to see the scientific equations rendered lifelike. For some patrons, only these complicated calculations mattered anyway. Algorithms had become comforting to people, like a secret code, micro-targeted on their soul. Combining science with the images created a gravity in the room that pulled in even the most hardened skeptic.

Marcelo crafted a program that began running the moment a customer, solicited specifically, booked a seance. Once they unlocked the privacy controls in place, Marcelo could mine their data for the reading, along with his own growing collection of information. The released details influenced a complex set of factors deciding everything from the ritual's progression, the look of the room, the touch of fabric, even Marcelo's own dress and affectations. People had come to expect such high quality in the three years he'd been reading the fortunes of the deceased in alternate universes.

"Now, I see that we are here tonight to contact a lost loved one; so very sad when they are taken from us too soon." The shy family, hushed in reverence, took their places around the table. A father and two daughters solemnly regarded the fifth chair, more ornate than their own. It remained empty.

"Mr. Marcelo, thank you for choosing us. You have no idea what this opportunity means to our family. These are my daughters, Kristen and Andrea," said the older man. The grave father looked tired. Dark half-moons cupped his reddened eyes.

"Welcome, Josiah, and welcome Kristen and Andrea," Marcelo said.

Marcelo had no hardened heart. He could see the grief was fresh with this family. They were a fill-in appointment for another client that wound up dying before his scheduled meeting. Even after three years, a patron's pain washed over Marcelo fresh each time. He wanted to provide comfort, so much so that he believed he did reach people in other universes; some days, it was the only thing that helped him get out of bed. On Marcelo's worst days, he caught himself pining for his holograms of lakes and storms to be real and his wife to be breathing calmly in a Vienna that wasn't reduced to rubble.

So Marcelo's mission became one of comforting and profit because he knew that fragile human psyches needed plausible fantasies to live in. Ignorance, to some degree, did turn out to be bliss. And people were willing to pay a handsome sum for that ignorance.

"Shall we begin then?"

Marcelo sat in front of his thin screen and started the seance, which resembled a dance. First, the hologram of the dead mother and wife appeared in the empty chair, and unison gasps rippled across the family seated before the image. The mourners around the table then stifled sobs.

Marcelo equipped the empty chair with a holographic generator of his own design that would allow the highest quality images of dead family members to be rendered lifelike in three dimensions- an amalgam of scoured images paired with AI nanotechnology to fill in the gaps. This brought the deceased to life and present at the reading table. Marcelo relished the surprise every time. Customers usually gasped at the sudden appearance of their lost loves, then quickly warmed to the spectacle as if it were real. Our biology was fragile, Marcelo knew this intimately, and attuned to so many phenomena that self-deception became necessary to keep it all running.

Having started the reading calculations, Marcelo watched the youngest daughter reach out a hand to touch the image; she pulled it away when the flurry of nanoparticles tickled her skin.

With a flourish, Marcelo raised his arms and commanded several holographic floating blobs into a pattern that grew to a large oval shape, like an egg on its side. His hands shaped the clumps like bread dough into a uniform whole as his body swayed with the energy of the room. The low gurgle of the storm and the lake's waters were a musical accompaniment to the performance.

The blue-tinted egg was a complex rendering of aggregate information of the known universe. It looked like a transparent globe that expanded and contracted with Marcelo's hand movements. The egg's oval presented a scale model of the cosmos, the entirety of all existence, in three dimensions. It was Marcelo's most sacred moment to consider the raw emotion of human loss juxtaposed with a vast unflinching void mostly filled with nothing. That is why Marcelo colored it blue instead of black and filled it with fiery gases left over from the Big Bang. Not many people could accept the void unconditionally. They shrank back from their own insignificance as they wallowed in grief and pain. It was too much to bear.

Equations were projected outside the orb. With these, Marcelo was able to calculate what he called "certain-lifes," which was the probability that a dead person was still alive in any number of alternate universes running parallel to our own. This was the part of the séance people paid top dollar for.

"I only wish to comfort those in need, nothing more," Marcelo nearly sang. "I will need you to follow me to another place. Will you?" The family nodded in unison. "Come with me," Marcelo beckoned the mourners. The family of three leaned closer with open faces. "I want to show you the infinite beyond our universe. I want to show you where the dead are still alive!"

Buzzing along the outside of the orb were complex strings of numbers. Marcelo's clients could follow certain bands chosen prior to their visit, which explained the life and adventures of an alternate version of a dead spouse or lost child. Some more frivolous clients could pay for a teenager's lost pet to be found prancing through another reality.

The same programs that created the room's different configurations and the hologram body in the ornate chair, also created possible *certain-life* paths for the dead based on choice options. Variables, such as if the dead walked straight on this day or turned left on the street instead of right the day they died, crawled along branches of time. Each certain-life had to be plausible. Marcelo marveled at the remaining biological human need for answers, matched with the subconscious defense against bullshit. Even in this advanced age, a subtle craftsman needed to reconcile fantasy with reality.

Marcelo's algorithm considered a data point set of variables for a certain-life that he chose early on in the program's construction. Based on data points like age, profession, genetic profile, method of death, and surviving family, he created probabilities in other universes. From those variables, fifty-two possible lives were chosen, and seventy percent of those were usually too similar to offer wonder, or excitement, for the family. They were eliminated based on points in life, like fingerprints, matching up with too much regularity.

Once the holographic settled on a certain-life, the hologram of the deceased explained the details of this new life, as if they had been summoned from the dead. Vocal recordings and videos swirled together to grant speech.

"Father, daughters, I'm pleased to tell you that I have located your wife and mother, and she is, in fact, still alive in this other plane, or what I like to call "alternate nows." Marcelo watched the three take deep breaths, awaiting more details of this second life. Then the hologram spoke:

"You're all here!" The vision of the dead mother exclaimed. "I know you must miss me, but I'm here now, see?" The hologram lifted its palms. "Tell me, what is it like there?" Those around the table remained silent.

"Go ahead, dears, speak to your mother," Marcelo prompted. Kristen was the first to speak.

"Mom, hi, um. Things are—we miss you so much. I love you." Marcelo had seen this awkwardness many times. It took some warming up for the family to accept what they were seeing. Acceptance and reality weren't always kind bedfellows, Marcelo mused. Which brought about a unique challenge that tested Marcelo at every seance.

How do you include those around the table in a certain-life? Another program became necessary to incorporate data points of those around the table, the living. Marcelo found a way to make the clients players in the certain-lifes. Using their own cached information, he inserted their likenesses into the bands of the chosen hologram. Most people grew overwhelmed seeing themselves in certain-lifes. Marcelo hoped for this to bury deeper into their real minds and solidify the transcendent experience he was selling.

"Darling, it is so good to see you again. I needed to tell you that I finished building the house. If only you could see it," Josiah said. Marcelo sprang into action at his cue.

Flourishing his arms, he zoomed into the outer blue egg with a grand sweep of his hands. The hologram buried down to the surface of the alternate Earth. Marcelo's view came to rest, over the shoulder of the deceased. Each family member took a deep breath and leaned forward.

"I built for us a home too; all four of us live in such a beautiful place now," said the holographic mother.

"Your mother chose a slightly different path in this world, but amazingly she still brought forth two daughters," Marcelo added. "Your names are different, and the color of your eyes has switched. You, the youngest, are now the oldest." Marcelo gave the women time to consider these variables. "And her dear husband, I see for you a career change; it looks as if you became an artist in this reality, making beautiful wooden sculptures. Look! And, your departed love has such a vibrant life building houses! The two of you work together in this life to build homes and decorate them. What by chance did your wife do here in our universe?" Marcelo asked, knowing full well what the answer would be.

"She sold homes, but never built them. How lovely that she's using her hands again—then, or, wait, I—uh—" The husband looked on excitedly, tripping over his own thoughts. Marcelo leaped to the next phase, which was to manipulate the holograms inside the large egg of the universe to give the clients an indelible visual.

"Now that I have located her in the certain-life, let me show you some of her homes and handy work." Marcelo paraded a host of 3D images across the table, and the family marveled at the ornate homes their other mother built in the other world. "My calculations are a bit fuzzy now; the complexity of all this seeing into other worlds can cause hiccups in the machines. I see some words inside one of the houses; it looks to be a kind of message."

This was Marcelo's ultimate breathtaker. He called it the "phone call from another world." He programmed the hologram chair rendering to look at the family and smile. He made the woman lean forward with a subtle parting of the lips, making the dead mother look like she were about to speak.

"It looks as if there is a message for you here, something that crosses the boundaries of the universes. Your mother seems to be saying something, it's dark, and she looks to be on her knees praying now. Did she ever pray?"

Josiah smiled.

"That wasn't prayer; every night, she'd sit like that and talk to me with her elbows on the bed. I remember lying there, and she told me about her day."

Marcelo reviewed some notes quickly as his calculations had missed an important distinction, some truly private data. He moved a few details around quickly, found a less religious quote, but the certainty percentages weren't substantial. He could be at risk of losing the group's suspension. The seance was nearly finished, and a few false words could ruin the spell he cast.

"Let me make an adjustment here," Marcelo paused, then

flourished his arms. "I can see her now, on her knees, but she is in another part of the house." Marcelo began to sweat. What on earth could the woman be saying? The program had hit a loop with the new information, which could take minutes, if not hours, to cycle through. The infinite possibilities had a ceiling, a Marcelo-imposed limit, but even under his limits, the variations became labyrinthine. Marcelo knew of only one thing to say. He'd uttered it to himself only once before. It was not part of any calculation.

"The message is small; it's coming through in fragments." Marcelo adjusted the light of the hovering egg. A somber blue hue made the hologram shrink. All three family members leaned closer to the table for the message spoken by the dimming hologram. Marcelo struggled to release those long-lost words. He didn't want to give them away again. He felt the weight of the fake room shrinking into him as he fumbled. He had only one real comfort to give anyone, and selfishly he'd kept it to himself all these years. He hadn't been able to say it in time before the bombs fell.

"You fit with me here and nowhere else," spoke the hologram mother. These sacred but unspoken words to Anya flooded the room with red light. Marcelo planned it that way for himself alone. But the effect through the room was palpable.

"You see," said Marcelo. "No matter where you are, you are with her. No matter *which you* you are, she is with you." His words rang like a prayer.

All three patrons became still lifes on the other side of the table. Marcelo could see their shocked faces through the glowing blue egg. The grieving husband had shimmers of light wiggling in his eyes. The two daughters looked to their father in disbelief.

Marcelo could see one woman was near fainting. He took a deep breath and moved from his seat around the table with a grand gesture. He placed two warm palms on the woman's shoulders. The press of his hands helped to release the tension that held her rigid. She collapsed, but Marcelo caught her, and the others moved to recover her further.

The Great Marcelo stood near the door to his small bungalow of technological marvels and watched the family leave in their vehicle. He repeated the line in his head, "You fit with me here and nowhere else." Perhaps it was something the father needed to hear, he thought.

* * *

Marcelo welcomed the next evening's clients with the sleek version of the room projected, full of glass, blue hues, and shiny surfaces. Two bored-looking men in plain suits and the third man in a military uniform sat before him in the seance room. They looked like a tough crowd to impress. Marcelo feared these people the most. Two reasons gave him pause when considering these types as clients: how influential they would be after the seance and how volatile their reaction would be if they did not get what they wanted. Their loyalty was equally as powerful, though—another calculated risk. Money, no matter its form, held the *worlds* in an iron grip.

What Marcelo knew was that not only did the volatile types book him for that very evening, but the family of the two plainly dressed men had crucial ties to the military finance industry. Finally, a customer he actually couldn't say no to.

Marcelo's talents had become so well known that the government sought out his services.

"Come, please, sit," Marcelo called. The three made their way from the vestibule of the small shop and into the hologram room. Marcelo removed every amount of kitsch that had been set out for the father and daughters the night before. The still, quiet, and clean room presented the group with no frills or distractions. The military man was impressed, and the other two patrons continued to look disaffected and bored.

"So, let me pull up your profiles," Marcelo spoke plainly. "I've taken the liberty of culling the results of the search, as is customary. There are infinite possibilities, so eliminating a large swath of results as too similar to this world merely makes for a more productive evening."

The three men looked on silently. Marcelo remarked that even when excitement showed on these war-hardened types' faces, it seemed tinged with a hint of irony as if they didn't believe what they were seeing was real, protection against possible deception. It was also below their status to be tricked into an emotional response. These were the clients Marcelo never touched with his own hands. Touching them would only serve to take precious warmth away from himself for nothing.

Marcelo began, and the men watched the hologram display with detached stares. Mathematical charts made of projected light were stacked in a unique configuration that Marcelo made a great show of wiping away. No matter what their affectation, customers always enjoyed a little flourish of the dramatic. Marcelo noted that each man followed the floating images of crumpled papers as they disappeared into the air.

"You made a special request, Admiral, and I have had a most enjoyable time in the hunt for your query. I used the following calculation to find the likelihood that your mother is still alive on another plane, and I have located her. Here, I have written the calculation." Marcelo traced symbols with his finger, and they appeared over the hologram of a house he found in several pictures of the Admiral's mother's cache profile.

$$N = R^* \times Fp \times Ne \times Fl \times Fi \times Fc \times L$$

"Would you care to hear from her, or would the details suffice?" The three-member group looked at each other and nodded in agreement. Marcelo waited for one of them to speak.

"We have decided we would like another person found, I mean, reached," the military man said. Marcelo's pulse increased

25

slightly; he hadn't anticipated such a request. Then the admiral produced an antique firearm, laying it down on the seance table. The contours of his chiseled face reflected as much light as the room did.

Marcelo began to open his mouth in protest, but closed it abruptly when he considered the firearm. He knew what those brutish weapons could do to a delicate room such as his. Or to delicate flesh. Diligently he set about calculating a new profile with the habitual motions of his hands.

"We have someone we'd like to see," one of the plain men spoke. Marcelo broke into a light sweat because he never entertained on-the-spot requests. Information was gathered beforehand, usually in secret, and the deceased's profiles were created before the seance. It made a seamless narrative of his calculations. Marcelo had no desire to stray from his profession's charlatan traditions. But the three men stared at him with a bureaucratic sense of entitlement mixed with the gun's implied savagery.

Then Marcelo felt an uncanny sensation that he was being watched by other eyes. He tapped his foot on a sensor below the table to sweep the room for recording devices, but none were detected.

Nonetheless, he sat up straighter in his chair at the prospect of being surveilled and weighed the possibilities of saying no. He'd heard of people saying no to these types of men before. He'd also heard how those same people's loved ones may need his services for a "phone call from another world."

"Very well, gentlemen, who can I begin a search for?" The plain one who spoke produced a picture tablet. In it, a young woman was lying in the middle of the road. Part of her body was lodged beneath an automobile. She had a blank face, and small amounts of blood could be seen at the corners of her mouth.

"And who might this be?" Marcelo asked.

"I don't know," said the younger man. "She jumped in front

of me this morning." Marcelo looked down at the picture. He tapped his own recording device button below the table to record the image before the tablet screen went black, then the military man took the tablet back and closed it. Now Marcelo knew he was being tested. First the threat of the gun said, 'do as you're told,' and now a picture of some dead woman demanded his silence.

Marcelo's mind attempted the calculations of possibilities: perhaps the man wanted his guilt assuaged or maybe this woman was a spy. All this could assess Marcelo's abilities, forcing him to reveal himself as a fraud or a prophet. Both were dangerous.

"Well, let me try something on the fly." Marcelo remained calm but knew that several calculations would take an incredible amount of time to finish. He busied himself with swipes and points to the hologram generator, making a fabulous show of building the woman's profile in the picture. The real algorithms worked in the background to find the woman, her information, all based on a photo of her dead face. Marcelo kept close watch of the three men, stony, like poker players. He looked for any chink in the steely armor of the man who never talked, and amid all the show, the fanfare of images, he found it.

The man who claimed to have hit the woman in his car looked sideways at the other gentlemen. Marcelo watched the quiet man, studying the flourishes of holograms. Behind his eyes lurked a panic seeing every image that flashed up of the woman. Marcelo confirmed this when he saw the man's forehead crease. His body visibly shakes at the woman's full hologram image appearing in lifelike high definition in the empty chair next to him.

"Holy Christ!" The man yelled, then wiped his upper lip.

"I apologize for the surprise." Marcelo dimmed the image of the woman to a flickering shadow. His sleight of hand with the woman's appearance allowed him enough time to manage the elimination of ninety-nine percent of the profiles generated. He grew more uneasy when the one percent of profiles left revealed nothing, but that the woman had been killed in a hit-and-run earlier that day. He needed a viable profile, and she did not generate one.

So Marcelo settled on one. An Anya.

He knew it well, could recite it from memory. He uploaded the narrative to the nameless woman dead in the road. He was thrilled, as he hadn't been in a long time. He'd prepared this narrative years before as an alternative to the memorials of the bombing that took his wife. He'd never used it. It was his first Anya.

The profile was simple in its cruelty. The woman now reigned over a large town with impunity and savage malice that resulted in the torture and despair of thousands. The Great Marcelo made her a tyrant in another life to comfort himself, left behind in this one. It would suit to assuage the guilt of the quiet man, he assumed. It had assuaged his own. Marcelo let the main simulation play out as he continued to search for the real woman's information. His calculations ran continuously in the background as the three men soaked up the story Marcelo had created for his own wife after her violent death. This Anya bought him valuable time.

Of all the curiosities, technology, dramatic flourishes Marcelo knew, the woman in the road had been able to pull off the greatest trick. She did not exist in any information cache to which Marcelo had access. She was a completely anonymous human being. Each and every search Marcelo conducted came back with null results. This woman had left no trace of herself anywhere. It was an astonishing achievement that could only be realized with some new technology. But she was dead, silent now.

"Very odd that this woman you wanted me to locate seems elusive, even in other worlds," Marcelo mused. He knew full well that the men had tricked him. They already knew who she had been and that her entire existence had been scrubbed away. So what did they want with him? The discovery of loose ends?

All three men remained still as Marcelo finished his reading. This woman tyrant knew no love and had no confidant in this other world. She laughed at the writhing of her subjects. The quiet man spoke up with excitement in his voice.

"I found out that my wife worked for OPS helping people disappear. She knew about you too and how powerful your readings are. For ten years, I thought I knew her. Now I know what I did was right. Even on other planes, she was evil. I'm not sorry for what I did."

Marcelo sat horrified. The comfort he'd hoped to offer transformed into a justification for murder. He felt his wife die again. He looked at the large blue egg hovering above the table—infinite possibilities of cruelty and grace.

"I think what you have here will fulfill our needs perfectly," said the military man. "The science is as sound as it can be, and who would argue with this anyway? We've heard great things about your methods. Several top officials are eager to have a reading. We would also pay for the rights to the reading's results. The findings will be valuable pieces of evidence. I assume the information gathering you do can be, what should I say...adjusted? We'd need to have some input before you run the final numbers."

"Recalculated would be a better term to use," Marcelo said morosely. *You snakes*, he thought to himself.

"Yes, I like that. Your work will not only be a great display of our technology, but such a creative resource for the trackers to locate other OPS traitors. What a nice touch to make them less than desirable characters too. We will be back soon with an offer!" The military man tapped both palms on his knees and stood. Swiftly he holstered his antique sidearm and about-faced to leave.

Marcelo watched the men leave his parlor, knowing they wouldn't be gone long. His quiet life in the room would soon be co-opted by more powerful men, still in control of weapons and probably looking to use his seances in tradecraft around the smoldering globe. The quiet man looked back before rounding the corner. He waved at Marcelo and smiled.

That grin exposed yellow broken teeth.

"You. You vile pestilence," Marcelo hissed. "People like you killed her. And now you're killing her again. What have you made with your bombs and your spies? Rubble! That's it. And my Anya. She's not here with me because of you. She's there," Marcelo shouted. He pointed back to the reading room's cold, shiny surfaces. The men stared him down with complete indifference. The quiet man's smile disappeared into a sour look of pity and disdain.

"Monsters!" Marcelo lunged at the admiral and reached for the firearm at his side. He'd never used such a weapon, so when he pulled it from the holster at the admiral's hip, he discharged a round into the hologram room. A large crack in the hologram reflectors splintered outward from the hole.

Before he could fire another round, the military man rested the gun from his hand and fired once into Marcelo's gut. He doubled over in his long ornate robes and inched back into his seance room. The pain washed over him in waves.

"Didn't we need him to run it?" asked one of the suits.

"No, we can run all this without him. He's just here for the show," sneered the admiral. All three men left Marcelo to bleed out in the reading room, but he knew what to do.

Marcelo had one last Anya to deploy. The butterfly. He set the program to fly through all the algorithms and change tiny details throughout the millions of lines of code. It would take them years to unravel, and only he knew the rescind command —his precious words to her.

"You fit with me here and nowhere else."

Marcelo returned the room to the patio configuration with great effort, then shifted the image of the dead woman to that of his dead wife. She presided over her lost kingdom like a god; her appearance illuminated Marcelo's tired face. He might see her soon, and this comforted him. Then storm clouds rolled over the walls.

JUSTICE

By Sammi Caramela

I believe I was called here for a reason. I'm always believing things like that.

Missed my train and was late for work in Boston? The universe must be protecting me from an impending crash. Woke up sick the day of my first vacation in years? Perhaps something sinister had been awaiting me at the hotel I'd booked.

Got cheated on by my boyfriend of five years and had to move into the first apartment I could find, in some middle-of-nowhere Hallmark town in a state I've never even thought of visiting?

Must be fate.

I wasn't always like this—wasn't always bright and cheery and "everything happens for a reason." I'm still not. I'm not some toxic-positive, bullshit-spewing, naive soul who dresses her demons in pink. I'm a realist, but I'm also a believer.

If you choose to believe you're where you're meant to be, you won't waste time grieving the past you knew and the future you created in your head.

I settle in the grass at Round Valley Reservoir, digging my heels into the dirt as I fish my journal out of my backpack. I've heard many things about this place. "New Jersey's Bermuda Triangle" is another name for it, apparently. But it's also been deemed a "spiritual healing ground," at least by some random commenter on the Weird NJ post I read.

It's still evening; the sun hasn't quite set yet, though I can see the moon on the horizon. Lighting up a joint I rolled before coming here, I open my journal and click my pen.

Saturday, October 7, 2022

It's chilly today. Halloween's charm is looming over the town, gusts of wind ripping bright leaves off the trees.

When Augustine left me for his high school sweetheart, my first thought was to escape to New York. What better place for an artist, right? I could start over, meet some handsome writer in a coffee shop, become famous, and make anyone who's ever wronged me regret it.

Wrong. Unless you're looking to live with three randos, a couple of mice, and a family of roaches in an apartment the size of a closet, still barely making ends meet each month, New Jersey is your closest bet.

Plus, I'm not that kinda girl—the kind who seeks revenge. I usually just run away instead. I'm still trying to figure out why it's so easy for me to do that. My lack of emotional reactivity is kind of freaking me out…

But anyway. I did what I do best and ran from Salem. Ran away from all the years Augustine and I lived there together, all the memories we made. Away from the Salem Witch Trial documentary I had spent months on.

Despite all my knowledge of Salem's history, I still could never quite connect with it. And if an artist cannot connect with the location of her own film, it is bound to fail.

I'm still writing streams of consciousness as a bright green light shines directly on my paper. My first instinct is to put out my joint. I look up, expecting to see a police officer standing over me with some sort of flashlight.

But there's no one there.

Sure enough, a glowing ball of…*something* hovers directly ahead of me, almost as if it were floating on the water.

"What the…"

Neither the sun nor the moon could compare to the light cast by this burning green object.

I stand up, neglecting my bag and journal on the ground, and walk closer to the water, pulling out my phone to capture the incident. But as I'm about to press "record," the light flashes so brightly that I drop my phone in the reservoir, just before the light disappears over the trees.

"Fuck!" I step into the murky water to retrieve my phone, but I can't find it anywhere.

"Don't bother looking."

The voice comes from behind me, and I turn around to see an older woman watching me. She's wearing a black blouse tucked into a long skirt that reaches her ankles.

I smile at her, despite my unease. "Yeah, I think it's a goner."

"Everything that falls beneath that water's surface is a goner."

I blink. *Oh-kay.*

"Did you see that light?" I ask her, drying my hands on my jeans.

The lady smirks at me as if she knows something I don't. "You keep coming here, you'll see lots of things, my dear." She points out at the water, and I turn to follow her gaze. The forest along the edge of the reservoir is a portrait of autumn, reflecting reds and oranges and yellows onto the water.

"There's a whole village down there," the lady says.

"What do you mean?" I turn back to her, but she's gone. Just like that.

I look around, and the entire place is empty now. There are no cars in the parking lot, but I could've sworn there were at least three others when I got here. I didn't hear them leave.

Suddenly, the sky turns a threatening gray. The wind picks

up, tousling my hair.

Though chills spread down my arms and legs, I can't help but feel a flicker of excitement: *I just found inspiration for my next film.*

* * *

I have no phone, so I'm not sure how I'm supposed to get home considering I don't know my way around here. Retracing my path and following signs along the main road, I finally make it back to my neighborhood.

As soon as I get inside my apartment, which is decked with unpacked moving boxes, I toss my backpack to the floor and collapse onto the couch, loading the YouTube app on my TV. Using the remote, I type in "Round Valley Reservoir history." There are a few documentaries on the results page, so I click the first one and settle in.

It's gonna be a long night.

I order pad thai from my laptop and grab my notebook and a pen as the documentary starts. By the end of the evening, I have pages of scrambled notes, including:

- *Within five mins., a storm came over the dam, knocked over the rowboat, anchor got stuck.*
- *Late 1950s. Used to be small town with lots of farms, flooded it for drinking water, eminent domain, state bought the property and flooded it, farming community.*
- *People sinking into the mud...???*
- *Once was a popular Native American hunting ground and revolutionary war hangout.*
- *"Drowned Valley Reservoir."*

As I brush my teeth and wash my face before bed, I stare at my reflection in the mirror above my sink. The glass is dirty and streaked. I should probably wash it tomorrow.

My eyes look dull as they stare back at me, no longer a bright shade of brown that Augustine would deem "golden" in the sunlight. They look lifeless. *I* look lifeless. My tan is fading, my auburn hair is thinning from the stress.

I shake my head to break out of this superficial spiral. I have more important shit to worry about than my appearance.

As I crawl into bed for the night, some trashy reality show playing in the background, I feel a budding sense of purpose again. I have a story to tell. I have victims to do justice. I have theories to prove. I have…

"To be careful."

I jolt up in my bed, my heart in my stomach, searching for the source of the voice in my room.

"Hello?" I manage.

An older woman with the figure of a witch saunters through the doorway of my room, her bare feet dragging slowly across the floor.

She stops at the foot of my bed, stiff as a cardboard cutout. "You have to be careful."

I'm frozen, half my body still under the covers, shaking. I grab my glasses from my nightstand to see her better, and instantly, it hits me: she's the same woman from Round Valley.

"What are you doing here?" I ask her.

She sits on my bed, and I can't seem to move. It's like when you're in your dreams trying to run or scream, but your legs won't work and your mouth won't open.

Suddenly, a gust of wind picks up so loudly it sounds like a tornado is heading straight for my apartment. My power goes out. It's pitch black for a good five seconds before it flashes back on, and the woman is gone.

*　　*　　*

I park on the street in front of the coffee shop downtown, which is nestled along a river, string lights cozying up the place.

It's 8 a.m. on a cloudy Saturday morning, and I'm one of

the only people in the shop. The sound of the espresso machine calms my nerves.

"Good morning," I say to the baristas, inhaling the scents of bacon and coffee.

"Hey, Willow!" The small, curly-haired barista, who introduced herself as Rose the first day I came in here a week ago, greets me. "You're here early."

"Yeah, I had a...*strange* night last night. Didn't sleep much."

She gives me a sympathetic look, probably thinking I'm referring to a bad date or some other superficial reason to be in a bad mood. "Vanilla chai?"

I smile and nod. "Wow, it's only been a week and I already have a usual."

"What can I say? We're a small community." Rose leans in. "Also, don't look now, but this dude who comes in here all the time is sitting back there. Was totally checking you out."

I feel myself blush, but I am too fresh off my breakup to even consider flirting with someone new right now.

"So you said you had a weird night, huh?" the male barista, Ben, asks as he preps my latte. His long hair is tied back into a ponytail.

I pay for my drink, making a mental note to start buying black coffee. *I can't keep draining my savings account like this.*

As I wait, I explain my past twenty-four hours to Rose and Ben, including my trip to Round Valley, the bright flash of light I saw, and the storm that rolled in as if out of nowhere.

"Long story short, I lost my phone in the reservoir, so I have to get a new one this morning," I say. "Hence why I'm here so early."

I don't mention the lady at the reservoir. Or my dream. At least, I'm telling myself it was a dream.

"Round Valley is an interesting place," Ben says. "Lots of history, conspiracy theories, and such. You're not the first one to say they've seen a UFO."

Is that what I saw? I mean, I know the documentary quoted a lot of UFO sightings, but how can I be so sure that's what it was?

It's not that I don't believe in that kind of stuff. I guess I've just never really experienced it firsthand.

"I did a ton of research on the area last night," I tell him. "I'm actually planning on filming a documentary about it."

"A documentary about Round Valley?" a guy asks from behind me.

I turn around to see a guy maybe a little older than I am, in dark jeans and a black denim jacket. His bright green eyes pierce through me in a way I can't explain. I feel like he's looking deep into my past or something.

"Sorry, I didn't mean to eavesdrop," he adds. "I'm Kris. I'm a writer. Well, a journalist. I've done an editorial on Round Valley for a local magazine. Learned a lot of crazy shit about that place."

"I don't doubt that," I say, wondering if he wrote one of the articles I devoured last night. "Seems like that place has some sort of curse on it."

"That's not even half of it."

"That's awesome you're into film," Rose says to me. "I *knew* you were cool."

I laugh, caught off-guard. "No one's ever called me 'cool' before."

Ben hands me my drink. "Sounds like you're hanging around the wrong people then," he says.

I smile, unsure how to respond to this level of attention and kindness.

"If you're gonna do this documentary, you shouldn't do it alone," Kris says as I start to walk away.

Something about the way he says it makes my blood boil.

I turn back around to face him. "Why's that?"

"There's a lot you don't know. A lot you're gonna find out. And doing it alone, especially as...well..." He trails off, leaving me to fill in the blanks.

If only he knew the shit I've already been through.

"I don't scare easily," I tell him.

He shrugs. "Well, if you change your mind...I don't want to intrude, but I do know a lot about that place, as I said. Maybe I can help you parse through some of the facts and myths. Make sure you do the place—and its victims—justice."

I blink at him.

"No pressure," Kris adds quickly. "But if you run into any sort of danger, please give me a call." He hands a piece of paper with what I'm assuming is his number scribbled on it.

"Do you usually have your number ready for women at the coffee shop?" I ask.

"I mean it," he insists. "There's a lot you don't know."

*　　　*　　　*

Round Valley is crowded this afternoon, with families picnicking on their blankets and lovers cuddling on benches by the water. My heart tugs with a sense of longing, being here alone. But I try not to dwell on it. What good does that do?

Growing up in foster care, I've learned a thing or two about letting go—of what should've/could've/would've been, of trauma, of people. Augustine was the only person in my life who ever really knew me, who touched me with kindness rather than anger or selfish desire.

Now, he might as well be dead.

I release these unproductive thoughts and settle on the grass by the reservoir, setting up my equipment so I can record a timelapse video. My goal is to capture a storm, should it roll in like it did yesterday, or another flash of light (or, what many of the documentaries I watched last night mentioned, a UFO).

As I leave my camera to record, I write a script in my notebook that I can recite as narration, consisting of all the facts I learned yesterday during my research. This is possibly my favorite part of filming: setting the scene with words as much as with the actual scenery itself. Narration is a powerful element in a documentary. It creates intimacy viewers can't help but embrace.

Every decent documentary also includes interviews, which unfortunately means I'll have to talk to people.

It's not that I don't like people. I happen to find them intriguing. It's just that I don't know many people here, aside from my "friends" at the cafe.

I guess Kris wouldn't make the worst interviewee, either, given he's a reporter who's done extensive research on this place. Part of me doesn't want to call him, though. The part of me who is too proud to ask anyone else for help—especially someone who assumes you need it.

But I can't let that side of me hold me back from creating the most impactful documentary I can create—and that kind of film requires interviews.

So, I grab the crumpled piece of paper out of my pocket and call him on the new phone I bought this morning.

He shows up barely ten minutes later, as I'm still working on the narration for the documentary, assigning them to clips I plan to capture.

"I knew you'd call, but I didn't think it would be so soon."

I look up at Kris from where I'm sitting on the ground. He's holding a notebook, smirking at me.

"It's not too late for me to change my mind," I tell him.

Laughing, he settles down next to me. "Now why would you want to do that?"

I roll my eyes, knowing he's right: I don't know anyone else in this town. Thankfully, its Hallmark charm makes me feel comfortable enough to trust a complete stranger.

"I've been here all day and haven't caught a single thing. It's like whatever strange...*thing*...is here knows I'm trying to expose it."

He tilts his head at me. "Didn't peg you as the type to give up."

It strikes a nerve—the way he says it. Maybe because he's pegged me wrong: I've given up on most things in my life.

And because he met me for, like, two seconds. How would he have pegged me as *anything* in that short amount of time?

"You said yourself you saw some creepy shit here," he continues. "But a watched pot never boils, so they say."

"Do they say that?"

He shrugs. "My mom does."

I laugh, shaking my head. It's colder than it was before, with the sun starting to set, so I tug my sweatshirt sleeves over my hands and hug my knees to my chest.

"So, what do you want to know?" he asks me.

"Well, I guess I was wondering whether I could feature you in the documentary. Interview you, maybe do some voiceovers, some shots of you explaining the experiences you had while writing your feature."

He raises his eyebrows, amused. "You want me to be *in* your film?"

I shrug. "You can say no. I'll find someone else. I just thought —"

"I'm not saying no."

He looks deeply into my eyes, and I feel the same way I felt at the cafe earlier: like he can see me in a way no one else can. And not in the cliche romantic kinda way that builds chemistry and makes you want to jump the person.

Rather, in an invasive, semi-chilling, yet captivating way.

I break contact and tuck a strand of my messy hair behind

my ear, looking out at the water. It's getting dark quickly again, but not because of a storm this time. The sky is clear, the full moon rising. Closing my eyes, I inhale a long breath, imagining I'm absorbing some of the moonlight, its energy fueling me, grounding me in this very moment.

This has been an instinct of mine for years since I was a little girl in foster care. At night, I'd count my breaths and picture the full moon over my bed shining down on me, even though the room was always pitch black with no windows. And I'd breathe in, deep and slow, especially when I felt the mattress shift under my older foster brother's weight. And I'd breathe out all his toxicity once he left me alone, as if that somehow protected me from his wandering hands—creating a force of energy around me.

"Are you okay?"

I open my eyes to see Kris watching me. Quickly, I wipe the tears from my eyes.

I don't cry. I didn't shed a single tear when Augustine ended things. It's just not something I do.

Maybe this place really *is* a spiritual healing ground.

I ignore his question and stand up. "I think we should get to recording," I tell him. "It might look cool to interview you as the sun goes down, under the moonlight."

"You know this place closes after dark, right?"

I narrow my eyes. "Didn't peg *you* as the goody-two-shoes type."

"Oh, I'm not," he says, following me from the bench closer to the water. "I just figured *you* were."

"You've really read me all wrong."

He stops next to me, close enough that I can feel the warmth of his body. He looks down at me, his eyes like magnets to mine. I swallow the anxiety that's suddenly fluttering in my throat but keep my gaze locked on his.

"Why did you move here?" he asks me, his voice soft as a whisper.

"I thought *I* was the one asking the questions."

He doesn't falter. "Ask me anything."

Slowly, I lift my video camera and step away to capture him. I hit "record."

"You've written extensively about Round Valley," I start. "What originally motivated you to look into the conspiracies surrounding this place?"

"I grew up here. I've always known it to be a strange place, though it's basically a second home to me. Or used to be, at least."

" 'Used to be?' Why not anymore? Has all the dirt you dug up caused a change in heart?"

He pauses, his face going dark for a moment. "You could say so."

"What did you find most disturbing about Round Valley?"

"That what they say is true—it really lives up to its name of 'New Jersey's Bermuda Triangle.' "

"How so?"

"Well, for one thing, twenty-six people have disappeared here." He runs his hand over the dark scruff on his chin. "In many cases, it remains a mystery. Most of the victims got sucked underwater somehow. One of them even resurfaced years later, glasses still on his face, his body still intact, for the most part. No good explanation for that one."

Kris looks out at the water. The sun is barely casting any sort of light, just enough for the sky to glow a deep blue. Wispy clouds float on the horizon, briefly covering the moon as they glide across the scene.

"What's most disturbing is that when one body surfaces, another disappears." Kris shakes his head sadly. "It's devastating. All the families who have lost a loved one here."

"Have you spoken to any of the victims' families?" I ask him.

"What did they have to share?"

Kris hesitates. "You're speaking to one of them right now."

I lower the camera slowly, meeting his eyes. Suddenly, the confident, arrogant man I thought was standing before me looks more like an unsure little child.

"What do you mean?" I ask.

"I lost my brother to these waters."

*   *   *

Kris and I plan to meet at Round Valley again the next morning so I can interview him more while capturing more footage. We grab breakfast and coffee from the coffee shop downtown—Rose raises her eyebrows at me when she sees I'm with Kris—then head over to the boat launch where Kris's brother supposedly drowned.

"Are you sure you want to tell this story?" I ask him.

As someone who has fled the scene of every traumatic event I've ever endured, I can't imagine returning—over and over again—to the same place where you experienced the worst day of your life.

"This can stay between us, and you can just continue to share your insights in the interview," I offer.

"I'm positive. I want to share his story. I want to do him justice."

I set up my timelapse video on my phone again, in case anything weird happens, and grab my video camera to start interviewing Kris.

"Can you tell me about your brother? What was your relationship like?"

Kris pauses for a moment, staring out at the water as if he's lost in a memory. "He was my best friend. We did everything together. He was the better version of me, truly. He was two years younger, but I looked up to him like he was the older brother."

My heart aches for him, feeling his loss almost as if it were my own.

"What were you two doing here that day?" I ask gently.

"Well, it was just like any other day. We were early teens, fishing on the water in our boat. It was a bright and sunny autumn day, kind of like today. Then all of the sudden, out of nowhere, a storm comes rolling in. Dark clouds covered the sky so quickly, we didn't have time to even make it back to shore."

He pauses, his jaw twitching.

"We weren't that far out, of course, but it all just happened so fast," he says, wiping a tear as it rolls down his cheek.

I want to reach out to him. Grab his hand. Pull him against me. Make it better, somehow.

But I don't even know how to do that for myself.

"Before I knew it, our boat capsized," he continues. "It took me a few moments to figure out which way was up and which was down, to make it back to the surface for air. Once I did, I couldn't find Jeremy anywhere. That's his name, by the way. I'm not sure if I told you that before."

The wrinkles on his forehead somehow appear deeper than just a few minutes ago, as if talking about his trauma and grief aged him within seconds.

"But anyway, yeah, that was that. He just...disappeared. Never surfaced. I tried looking for him, but I swear to God, it was like he just wasn't there anymore. I searched for what felt like hours before finally calling for help."

"How did you make it back to shore?" It feels like a fucked up question once it leaves my mouth. Like I'm asking how he managed to neglect his brother in the water or something.

Kris shrugs. "I just swam, I guess. I don't even really remember. My adrenaline took over, and before I knew it, I was out of the water dialing 9-1-1."

"And the storm came out of nowhere?"

He nods slowly, running his hand through his dark hair. "Out of thin air, it felt like. And left just the same."

Exactly how it had happened the first time I came here.

"How long did it take for the police to get there?" I ask him.

He pauses, thinking. "I don't know, it's kind of hazy. I'd say ten, maybe fifteen minutes. Too long to do anything to actually help. It was too late. He was gone before I even made the call."

I picture Kris here alone, disoriented and terrified for his brother's life, knowing he was gone but still waiting for help to arrive. It must have been agonizing.

"What did they say when they arrived?"

"I honestly don't remember. I kinda just blocked it out after. The only thing I remember them saying is that this wasn't the first time someone was 'sucked under, never to resurface.' Those were his exact words."

I wince at the brutal honesty of that statement. That's an insensitive fact to tell someone who'd just lost his brother.

A surge of anger jolts through me—the desire to protect Kris from the pain he'd already endured.

"It's okay," Kris reassures me as if he can read my mind.

I shake my head, wiping the tears from my eyes. "It's not."

He smiles sadly. "I'm just happy you're letting me tell my story. *Jeremy's* story."

*   *   *

I've spent nearly every day this week with Kris, capturing shots of Round Valley, hiking through the woods, smoking by the water, and interviewing strangers (thanks to Kris's extraversion). Never have I felt this connected to a creative project, and never have I worked so hard on it. At this rate, I'll be able to complete it in time for New Jersey's spring film festival, which Rose has encouraged me to enter.

After packing up for the day on Friday night, Kris asks if I want to grab drinks with him.

We haven't hung out outside of filming. The only place we've spent time was at the cafe grabbing coffee and sandwiches before heading to the reservoir for the day. The idea of sipping a glass of wine next to him at the bar and talking about anything other than the documentary creates a warmth in my chest I wasn't expecting.

"Let's do it," I tell him, getting into my car as he gets into his truck. "I'll follow you?"

"Sounds good!"

We always drive separately. I'm not stupid enough to let someone I just met know where I live, to pick me up and drive me around like we've been best friends for years. Augustine didn't even see my college apartment for the first six months of our relationship.

The local bar is packed with men in camo hats and large T-shirts. It smells like cheap beer and sweat when we walk in—not exactly the intimate setting I'd been imagining, but I haven't exactly been raised in high-class environments, so it kinda feels like home to me.

As we settle in two cramped seats at the corner of the bar and order our drinks, I make eye contact with a pretty brunette waitress who looks on the verge of tears as she darts from table to table. A few men old enough to be her father quite literally turn around in their seats to watch as she passes by, and they're not staring at her chocolate brown eyes. I can't help but feel a surge of protectiveness.

"You alright?" Kris asks me.

I turn my attention back to him just as the bartender approaches us with Kris's beer and my glass of red wine. Instead of answering him, I clink our glasses together and down a few sips of my wine.

Kris narrows his eyes at me, a smirk tugging at his lips. The way he studies me makes it feel like we're the only two in the room.

"What's your story, Willow?"

I laugh. "My *story?*"

He nods. "We all have one. You know mine. What's yours?"

"I'm gonna need you to get a little more specific with your questions," I say, taking another sip of my wine.

"Okay, I'll just repeat the question I asked you the first day we met: Why did you move here?"

I draw my finger along the condensation on my glass, somehow tuning out all the noise around us. "I got dumped by my boyfriend of five years."

He nods slowly, as if processing my statement. "Where'd you live before that?"

"Salem."

"Like, Massachussetts?"

"Is there another Salem?"

"There's one in Jersey, yes."

"Oh. Well, not that one. The witch one."

He laughs. "So...you came to Clinton, New Jersey specifically?"

I shrug. "I wanted to live in New York, but I'm an artist, so obviously I don't have the budget for it. And I don't do roommates."

"Why not?"

I shrug. "I like my solitude."

He nods again. "Well, Clinton is a nice town. I'm shocked you found an affordable place here though."

"Yeah, well, my landlord was the first to call me back out of the dozens I contacted in surrounding areas. Rent's *a little* higher than I'd wanted, but doable. I just needed out of my place in

Salem."

"You didn't have family you could stay with?"

I shake my head.

"I'm sorry to hear that."

"It is what it is."

"I mean, sure, but...I'm sorry *it is* that way."

I look Kris in the eyes and can tell he means it, which feels nice.

It's not that a man has never shown me empathy before. Augustine was a good guy. Honestly, if it hadn't been for him, I'm not sure I would have pursued my degree in film. He's the only person I've opened up to, and I'm lucky to have had someone who really listened to me. Who really cared.

I can say he's a prick for leaving me for another woman, but really, I'm just as much to blame. "Detached" is the exact word he'd use during our arguments toward the end. My emotional unavailability drove him right back into the arms of his first love.

I don't hate him for it. How could I? You can't commit to a ghost.

"Did you have a falling out with your family or something?" Kris asks.

I like that he isn't afraid to pry. There's nothing worse than someone tip-toeing around the truth as if you're too fragile to handle it—when you're the one who had to survive it in the first place.

"I never really had a family," I admit. "My dad left before I was born. My mom was struggling with addiction. Her parents were dead. I was in and out of foster care for most of my life, never in a permanent home. Once I went off to college, that was that. I met my ex junior year, and we built a life together in Salem after we graduated. Then he got back with his ex, I moved out, and here I am."

Kris stares at me for a few beats, as if he's taking everything in. I hold his gaze, daring him to ask more, but content with the silence that lingers between us. Communication isn't always verbal.

"What was it like in foster care?" he asks after a few beats.

I try to think of the right word. "Unstable."

"Did you get close to any of your foster siblings or parents?"

"Not really."

"Is there a reason for that?"

"There are a lot of reasons for that," I say carefully.

"What are they?"

I shift in my seat, finally breaking eye contact as the bartender walks over and asks if we want a refill. I order another glass of wine while Kris asks for a glass of whiskey.

"You don't have to tell me why," Kris says once the bartender walks away.

"There was a lot of abuse," I say, suddenly feeling exposed, yet oddly okay with it. "From the adults and the other kids. I did get close to one of my older foster sisters, but we got separated when I was eleven and she was fourteen, which destroyed me. I vowed to never get close to another sibling again."

Or anyone, really.

Maybe that explains my whole "emotional unavailability."

"I'm sorry, Willow," Kris says. "I hate to think you had to go through all of that alone."

He places his hand on my knee, somehow warming my entire body. I take a long, deep breath, finding his eyes again. They study me carefully, with intention, and I completely lose track of our conversation. Of my surroundings. Of my mind.

"Do you want to get out of here?" I ask him.

*   *   *

On Saturday morning, I settle at a table by the window, sipping my latte as I sort through all my footage with my AirPods in. I'm on a high from last night with Kris, giddy in a way I've never experienced—even with Augustine.

I'm not ignorant enough to get excited about us. Not that there even is an "us" to be excited about. But I *am* excited that I've been able to feel a desire strong enough to let some walls down —to open up to someone who doesn't try to fix what I've been through but rather creates a space where I can release it.

You can't understand someone else's darkness unless you've lived without light yourself. And Kris has certainly lived without the sun for quite some time. I can see it on his face as I listen to him tell me all about his brother in the video on my computer.

I edit clips and play with a few voiceovers for what feels like minutes but is more like hours when I get the sudden urge to search for Kris's feature in the town newspaper. I've never even read it. He said it was only published in the physical newspaper and not digitally, but it's 2022 and there's just no way there's no digital copy on the internet at this point. Maybe I can grab some more information—some details he left out.

A quick Google search brings it up right away. I click the link to the newspaper's site, but there's a different name under the byline. "Jeremy Nichols."

My blood turns cold.

I click on Jeremy's profile, and sure enough, the guy in the photo looks just like Kris.

But brothers can look identical, even without being twins. *Right?*

So...did *Jeremy* write this before he died?

Quickly, I click back to the article and read through it, my body shivering. All of the information Kris has told me lines up with the information in this article. The history of the place, the moments he spent researching the area, the fact that he and his dad would fish the reservoir most weekends growing up.

As I continue reading, I reach an interview with a local woman whose brother went missing in Round Valley a few years ago. Her story is identical to Kris's, except her brother's name was *Gus*, not *Jeremy*.

Just then, the door connecting the coffee shop to the antique store slams shut, causing me to jump. I take out my AirPods and look up to see what's going on.

It creaks back open slowly, and the owner of the antique shop, a petite, middle-aged woman with short blonde hair, peaks her head in. "She's been especially active lately," she says to Rose.

"Oh, I know," Rose says. "The other day, she threw a cup at my head!"

"Who did?" I ask them.

"The building ghost," Rose tells me.

"She messes with my shop all the time," the lady from next door adds, shaking her head as if with amusement. "Always making items disappear just to return them the next day, but upside down or out of place."

"You've seen her?" I ask.

"I have," Rose said.

I adjust in my chair, facing her. "What does she look like?"

She shrugs as the antique store owner returns to her shop, unbothered by it all. "Old."

The door slams again, causing us both to jump.

"BUT PRETTY," Rose yells to the ghost. She laughs, shaking her head. "She's harmless, but she's got some spunk to her, that's for sure. She commands attention."

"It's just her here?"

"She's the only one I've seen, but I've heard others speak."

"What do they say?"

"They'll just say 'hi' or 'excuse me.' Sometimes, they'll even say, *'BOO!'* to mess with me." The rest of the shop is empty, so Rose fixes herself a latte. "It's actually kind of funny. I've never felt scared of them," she says over the sound of the espresso machine. "They're good energy."

"This is crazy," I say. "I lived in Salem for years and never once experienced anything paranormal. Yet, I've been here for, like, two weeks and already have witnessed the wildest shit."

"Mmm, speaking of!" Rose says as she froths her milk. "How is your documentary coming along? You and Kris seemed to have been working pretty closely."

"Yeah, about that..." I contemplate telling her what I just stumbled upon. I do want to talk to someone about it, and I figure she's the closest thing I have to a friend here.

Other than Kris. Or should I say *Jeremy*?

Is that his name? Does he even have a brother?

"Do you know Kris well?" I ask Rose.

She shakes her head. "I mean, he's a semi-regular, but you'd know him better than I do." She leans against the counter, watching me. "I didn't even know his name till he introduced himself to you. Why?"

"I found something weird," I tell her.

"What do you mean?"

"Well, for one thing, I don't even know if his name is really *Kris*. And he told me his brother died at Round Valley. But I recently found the article he wrote about the place—at least, I think he wrote it, unless he has a twin—and the story he told me about his brother is verbatim the same story from his article, except it was told by someone he interviewed."

Rose goes quiet for a moment. "You mean, you think he stole his source's story?"

I sigh. "I have no clue. I don't know why he would do that. There'd be no reason to lie to me, but...the whole thing feels off to me. I mean, this is for sure him, right?"

I click on Jeremy's profile again, zooming in on his photo and turning my screen to Rose as she walks over to my table. She looks over my shoulder at my screen, eyebrows furrowed. "Unless he has a twin...that is for sure him."

"I mean, maybe he does?"

It dawns on me how little I know about Kris. And who's to say what I *do* know is even true?

A wave of anxiety mixed with rage washes over me. There's nothing I hate more than someone viewing me as gullible—and me playing into that narrative.

I should've been more careful, done more research. *I know better.*

"Lemme read the story," Rose says.

I click back, and she scrunches her face as she skims through. "This is a pretty specific story. Did he include the details about his—or her—brother's disappearance when he talked to you? Like he did in this story? Does the timeline match up?"

My head is spinning. "I have absolutely no idea."

"I guess there's only one way to find out," Rose says.

I look at her, questioning.

"You contact this girl."

❋ ❋ ❋

I type "Mariah Miller" into my Instagram search bar and click the first of many profiles. Thankfully, it's public, so I can scroll through photos of the girl who appears to be exactly the girl I'm looking for. Most of her photos are of hiking trails in the area; some are of her late brother, Gus.

I find one of her as a kid with two boys—who I assume to be her brothers—at Round Valley. The caption reads: It's not the same without you here, Gus.

The other boy in the photo is tagged. I tap it only to find his name is Kris.

Wait a minute. Is he...?

I click on the tag only to see the Kris in the photo is not *my* Kris. The Kris I've been spending time with.

Confusion swirls in my head like a shot of whiskey.

So, Jeremy is Kris.

And Kris is Mariah's brother.

And Mariah is Gus's brother.

And Gus is *not* Jeremy.

What the fuck is going on?

Frustration surges through me. I feel like I'm reading some shitty novel that name-drops ten characters in the first two chapters. I can't keep up.

I navigate back to Mariah's page and tap the follow button, then shoot her a DM:

Hi, Mariah. I know you don't know me, but I read an article, which you're quoted in, about Round Valley in the town newspaper. I'm wondering if you know much about the journalist: Jeremy? Strange story, but...essentially, he told me his name was Kris, and he is trying to pass off your story about your brother as his own for a documentary I'm filming. I want to make sure I don't spread misinformation in my film. I'm just really confused right now and would love to speak to you if you're comfortable doing so. I realize this is a lot, so if I'm overstepping at all, I will not be offended if you don't respond. And I will ensure not to include any stories I'm not 100% sure are true.

As I wait for Mariah's response, which I'm not sure will even come, I text "Kris" that I'm sick and won't be making it tonight.

Then, I hop in my car and head to Round Valley alone.

It's only five o'clock, but the sun is setting earlier and earlier each night. I'm the only one here when I show up. I want to capture that flash of light—the UFO—on video, so I get out of my car and head down to the water where I first saw it about a week ago.

"Leave."

I whip around quickly, slightly slipping on the gravel beneath my feet. As I catch myself, the old woman—the one from my first day, from my dream—stares back at me. Her long white hair falls over her shoulders, and her eyes are as dark as the night sky.

She looks angry, but I don't feel scared.

She stares at me from about ten feet away. I stare back at her.

"Leave," she repeats, her voice strong and steady.

"What do you want from me?" I ask her.

"Leave."

"Other than that, what do you want from me?"

Silence fills the air as the wind picks up. I cross my arms over my chest.

"Justice," she says softly.

"I am trying to bring justice to the right people. That's why I'm here." I step slowly toward her. "I think you can help me."

"LEAVE!"

She screams it this time, causing me to jump a bit. But I stay grounded, my feet firmly planted. "I'm not leaving."

I have nothing to say to her—only questions to ask. So I lift my camera and press record.

"What is your connection to this place?" I ask her.

But as I look through the lens of my camera, I don't see her anymore.

I lower the camera, and she's still standing there in front of me.

My heart drops. I open my mouth to speak, but before I can

get anything out, she yells, "LEAVE!"

Just then, the woman disappears into thin air—right before my eyes.

At the same moment, my phone pings with an Instagram DM from Mariah. I open the message immediately, my hands shaking so hard it's difficult to read.

Kris is my older brother's name...I have a feeling the man you are talking to is Jeremy. And if that's the case, you need to stop immediately and stay as far away from him as possible.

"Thought you were sick?"

I drop my phone on the ground with a loud thud.

"Is everything okay?" Kris—Jeremy—asks. "You look like you've seen a ghost."

I swallow my anxiety. For all Jeremy knows, I still think he's Kris. He's still the same guy I hooked up with the other night. The same man I opened up to at the bar. The same film partner I've been working with.

How did someone like me *get caught up in the whole "trustworthy small town" trope?*

I need to come off as nonchalant as possible.

"I'm fine!" I say. "I didn't want to miss a night of filming, but I also didn't want to get you sick, so I thought I'd come alone."

I go to grab my phone off the ground, but Jeremy places his foot over it.

My eyes lift slowly to meet his. His expression makes me shiver.

"Why have you been so quiet since we hooked up?" he asks, looking down at me.

I slowly stand back up, my legs suddenly wobbly. "I haven't been...I've just been busy working through the footage today."

"That's not true, and you know it."

"I don't know what you're talking about, Jeremy."

Fuck.

Realization washes over Jeremy's expression. He narrows his eyes at me. I hear my phone crunch beneath his weight. My eyes dart from my phone to his face, then over to my car in the distance.

I could run for it. I *should* run for it. What other choice do I have but to run for it?

But I'm paralyzed—the same way I used to be when my foster brother would sneak into bed with me. Too terrified to move. No longer in my body. Far, far above it. One with the moon, looking down at the scene below as it unfolds in slow motion.

"LEAVE!!!"

I hear the old woman ghost, but I don't see her this time. Instead, I see Jeremy folding over, hand on his gut, whimpering like he's been hit.

I take my chance to sprint to my car. My legs feel like lead, deadweights that somehow bring me forward, slowly but surely. I fumble with my keys as I hear Jeremy's footsteps behind me. I don't dare look back—I can only look forward.

I'm mere steps away from my car as I unlock it, just once, so only the driver's side unlocks. As I reach for the handle and tug the door open, Jeremy gets a hold of my arm and yanks me backward.

"No!" I yell. "Let go!"

He puts one hand over my mouth as I'm kicking and screaming for help. His other arm wraps around my waist so tightly I feel like my ribs are going to crack.

Suddenly, I'm back in my foster home with my older sister's arms wrapped around me from behind.

"If a man ever grabs you like this, you place your foot on their knee and drag your heel down their shin, then slam down on their

foot," she'd said to me. "Try it on me!"

I tried it, mimicking the movement gently.

"Good, but really do it this time," she said.

"I don't want to hurt you!" I cried.

"It's supposed to hurt, Willow. Just do it!"

It was the only time she yelled at me.

I hated being yelled at by her.

So, I did it. As hard as I could.

"Fuck!"

Jeremy's grip instantly loosens, and I somehow make it into the car, slamming and locking the door just before he reaches for the handle.

I throw the car into reverse as he slams his fists on the glass. My heart is pounding in my ears, my hands shaking. I speed away, my car kicking up dust in its path.

As I turn on to the main road, I see headlights creeping up behind me in the darkness. They get closer and closer as I speed up, and I know it's Jeremy, but I don't know how far he'd go. I don't know him at all, really. I don't know what he's capable of.

I'd call the cops, but I don't have a phone anymore. I'd drive to the nearest police station, but I don't even know where that is without directions.

Jeremy is so close to my car, I'm sure he's going to run me off the road. I'm going ninety in a forty-five, just praying for a police officer to appear and pull me over right now, but I don't even see any other cars on the road.

I can't go home. My only choice is to go to the coffee shop—somewhere public enough that Jeremy won't be able to get away with whatever it is he plans on getting away with.

I lay on my horn as I drive, trying to draw as much attention as possible as Jeremy bumps the back of my car.

"Shit!"

I try to keep my wheel steady and pick up the pace, but he keeps bumping me harder and harder as I drive. I can't possibly go any faster without completely losing control, so I slam on my brakes and rip my car down a country road, instinctively bracing myself for Jeremy to either side-swipe me or slam into the back of my car.

Somehow, I make the turn, my tires screeching in the process. My car slides a bit to the right, then a bit to the left as I try to recover. I don't see Jeremy's truck anymore, but I don't waste time looking for it. I continue down the side street and make it to the main road, then follow it all the way downtown.

Adrenaline parks my car, rips me out of it, and pushes me through the cafe entrance and straight up to the counter, where Rose and Ben are laughing with a customer.

"I need your phone," I manage.

"Woah, what happened?" Rose asks as I hear Ben say, "Are you okay?"

I imagine I look feral right now, eyes wide, panting like I just ran a marathon.

"Kris is not who he says he is," I tell them. "He tried to attack me. He tried to run me off the road. He could show up here any second. I need to call the cops."

Ben immediately grabs the phone as the customer eyes me like I'm some wild animal ready to bite.

"Hide her in the back," Ben tells Rose.

Rose puts her arm around my shoulder and guides me to the kitchen. "You're shaking," she tells me as she hands me a bottle of water. "Sip this. Do you want a warm drink? Cup of tea? Hot chocolate?"

I shake my head as I hear Ben on the phone with the police, relaying what I told him. The customers in the cafe are all asking what's going on.

A few minutes later, Ben appears in the kitchen, where I'm

sitting on the floor with Rose, hugging my legs to my chest. "Cops are on their way. I kicked everyone out and locked all the doors. You're safe here. I promise."

"It's gonna be okay," Rose echoes.

And for some reason, I believe them.

For the first time since Jeremy attacked me tonight, I start crying. For the first time *ever*, I break completely open.

✽ ✽ ✽

It's been a week since everything went down with Jeremy. After the police arrived and I explained the entire situation, they told me he'd been arrested for assault before. Turns out he's been accused of sexual and physical abuse by many women. He was even fired from the newspaper for that very reason.

Why he kept getting away with it is beyond me, but I'm going to make damn sure he never touches another woman again. And the officers promised me the same.

I sit in the corner at a table for two, sipping a chai latte as I wait for Mariah to show up. After Rose and Ben chipped in to help buy me another phone on Sunday morning, I contacted Mariah about Jeremy and asked whether we could meet up to talk about it.

I recognize her as soon as she walks in the door. She's a short, petite blonde with rosy cheeks and bright green eyes. Her hair is tied back into a tight ponytail, and she's wearing a sweatshirt and leggings with Converses. Casual, yet somehow put-together, she holds herself with a grace I can't help but envy.

"Mariah?" I ask, though I know it's her. She smiles and walks over, and I hand her the latte I bought for her when I got here.

"Thank you so much!" she says as she settles into the chair across from me. "It's so nice to meet you. I'm glad we're able to talk about all this, though I have to admit, I'm a little nervous."

Her vulnerability is admirable. A strength I lack.

"I'm nervous, too," I say. "Why don't I go first?"

She nods, and I explain everything, from my first day at Round Valley and meeting Jeremy at the coffee shop to the progression of our relationship and the way he attacked me.

"What's so weird about it all is that someone...a *ghost*, I believe...warned me, from the start. This lady just kept showing up, wearing the same outfit: a long-sleeved, black silk shirt and a long plaid checkered skirt. The entire time, I was afraid of her. But really, I think she was just trying to keep me safe from Jeremy."

"Wait a minute." Mariah pulls her phone out of her purse, her eyebrows furrowed together, scrolling down her own Instagram page. She taps a photo and shows me the screen.

On it is a picture of the woman I have been seeing everywhere. The ghost in my room, the lady at the reservoir. She's wearing the same outfit and everything, standing next to two teenage girls.

"That's her," I say.

"She was my grandma," Mariah says. "She lived in Round Valley before it was turned into a reservoir. That place meant the world to her."

Before I can even process this bit of information, I'm hit with another realization.

"Wait." I point to one of the girls in the photo, suddenly shaking. "Who is that?"

"Oh, that's my cousin! She's, like, my best friend. My aunt fostered her for a bit before officially adopting her."

Mariah must notice my expression, because she tilts her head at me, questioning. "Do you know her?"

"I used to. She was my foster sister."

"Wait...you're *the* Willow?"

I laugh in disbelief. "She talks about me?"

"*All* the time! Oh my gosh, she's gonna be so excited when I tell her about you. She only lives a town over, so I'm sure she'll want to see you."

I don't even bother to wipe the tears from my eyes as they glide down my cheeks.

"Wow," is all I can think to say.

Mariah smiles. "Yeah. I think we were meant to connect. I think that's what my grandma wanted."

"I think so, too."

We sit in silence for a few moments. I stare at the table, wondering how I got here, but happy I somehow did.

"Jeremy assaulted me," Mariah says suddenly. I look up and meet her eyes, quietly letting her know I'm listening. "After interviewing me, he tried to make a move. I shut him down, but he kept pushing. I felt so uncomfortable, so afraid, that I stopped fighting it and let him do what he wanted.

After, I told him to forget the article—that I didn't want him writing my story. A few weeks later, it was published. But I'd just wanted to forget about it. I didn't want to talk about what happened. I didn't want to talk to *him*. So I just let it go."

I wipe the tears from my eyes as she does the same.

"Then you messaged me, and I thought, 'If I don't speak up, he's gonna do the same thing to this girl,'" Mariah told me. "I wish I'd said something sooner."

"That's not your responsibility," I say. "You don't owe anyone your story."

She smiles sadly. "No, I don't. But if it can help others, I want to share it."

I place my hand over hers on the table, instantly thinking about my foster sister. The bond we had was so special to me. More special than any relationship I've had before. It carried me through life.

I thought I lost her forever, and so I stopped searching for that kind of connection with anyone, terrified to lose it again. Now, here I am, knowing she's just a short drive away from me. Here I am, sitting across from her cousin who feels like a long-lost friend. Here I am, at a small cafe in a random town in a state I never imagined living in, now friends with baristas who know my order by heart and support me like I'm their sister.

So many deem Round Valley Reservoir "New Jersey's Bermuda Triangle," and maybe it does live up to its name. But maybe two things can be true at once. Because it's also been a "spiritual healing ground." A place where bad things happen, but also a place where families create memories. A place of loss, but a place of gain. A place of mourning, but a place of loving.

I believe I was called here for a reason. I'm always believing things like that.

"Maybe we can share our stories together," I offer. "We can share Gus's story, too. All of it—the right way."

Mariah nods slowly. "I'd like that."

Though grief and sorrow flood my eyes, I can't help but feel a flicker of hope: *I just found inspiration for my next film.*

KILLING THE FUTURE

By Ellen Parry Lewis

"Oh my gosh. What is wrong with me?" I said aloud, wiping my teary eyes with the back of my hand. Ever since I found out I was pregnant, I had noticed a tendency to cry at arguably "non-cry-worthy" things. But crying at a children's cartoon was a new low for me.

I turned off the TV, stood up, and laughed just a bit. "What do you think, Cal? Is Mom losing it?" I said to my six month baby bump.

I was about to turn on some more lights as the sun was starting to set when I heard a knock at the door. Opening it, I saw a young woman standing outside, her hair draped down and over one of her eyes. "Can I help you?" I asked.

"Actually, I came to help you, Melanie," she responded, her only visible eye a piercing blue.

I cocked my head to the side. "Do I know you?" I asked, trying to place her and failing.

"You've met me before, but I'm sure you don't remember me. But we don't have time for that. I brought you something," she said, thrusting a small stack of papers at me.

The top paper was a printed-out news article with the headline: "Collingsboro Husband Allegedly Kills Pregnant Wife."

"What is this?" I asked. "A neighbor?"

"Not a neighbor," she said, roughly reaching out a hand and flipping to the next page. For a second, I was confused. There was a photo of me from just the month before. Mark had taken it when we had gone apple picking. I was standing sideways, my baby bump barely there. Then, I realized that it was the second page of the article.

"What is this?" I asked, staring at the stranger before me.

"We don't have much time," she simply said again, reaching out and thrusting the regular print edition newspaper onto the top of the pile. There was a similar headline and a picture of me and Mark at a restaurant for our anniversary a few months before. "Just in case you didn't trust the online copy," the woman before me said.

"I don't understand," I said, as she took a step past me and into the house. I numbly realized I should probably stop a stranger from walking inside, but she was so sure, and I was so confused.

"Look at the date," she said, closing the door behind her.

"November twenty-second. Isn't today the twenty-first?"

"Yes. But if you read the article, today is the day you die," she said, crossing her arms in front of her.

I took a step back from her. "What are you talking about?"

"I don't have time to explain," she said, impatiently rooting through her purse. "Mark will be home soon, right?"

"Yeah," I said slowly.

"When he comes home, he's going to kill you."

"You're crazy," I said strongly.

"No. I'm trying to save your life. You fight about things, right?"

"Every couple fights about things," I said defensively.

"Well, today's fight isn't going to end so well for you," she said, finding what she was looking for. She thrust out her hand to me. "You wear the green watch. I need the black one," she said, holding out what appeared to be a smart watch.

"What is this?" I said, not taking it.

"Just try this, okay?"

I still didn't move.

"Listen. As crazy as this must be for you, you have to believe me. I'm from the near future, and I'm trying to save your life before Mark gets home and kills you."

Somehow, that last bit was still the craziest thing she had said.

"Mark would never kill me."

"Well to prove that these articles and what I'm saying is true, I want to take you with me. Through time," she emphasized. "Just put on the watch. If it doesn't work, dismiss me as a lunatic, and I'll be on my way. But if it does work," she left the sentence unfinished.

I reached forward, rather eager to prove her wrong. And yet, I couldn't help but be slightly excited too. Things like this didn't happen in real life. Was I being recorded for some show or something? "The green one is for you," she said again as I touched the watches. "It's the lead device."

I put it on as she strapped on the black one. "Now, let's go back to a time when it still wouldn't be too traumatic, so think about when you first met Mark," she said. I played along and did as I was told for a few seconds. Then the woman instructed, "Now, while thinking about that time, put your finger on the top of the screen, like you're leaving a fingerprint.

A knock at the door interrupted my action. "Just do it," the girl practically yelled at me, and I touched the screen.

I let out a panicked, burst of a yell. The switch had been instantaneous. I found myself in a harshly lit fire hall. Groups of people milled about between cushioned, foldable chairs. And right in front of me was a young me and Mark. I knew the memory well. It was where my church had been temporarily meeting, the older building having recently burnt down. Mark had lived near the fire hall, and had come to visit the makeshift church with his family. We were both eighteen. He was telling me about his recent trip to Egypt. His brown eyes on me were excited. I was a little surprised by how much hair he had. His hair had noticeably thinned now in our late thirties, but I had forgotten how thick and dark it used to be. Meanwhile, I could practically sit on my brown, straight hair when I was that young. And when did I finally get hips, I wondered, staring at my impossibly stick-figurish body in front of me.

Yes, we were different and two decades younger, but seeing it before me, it felt fresh. My eighteen-year-old self was staring at Mark in wide-eyed wonder, and he was looking at me like I was the most captivating sight in the world. To say it was love at first sight would have perhaps been a bit much, but there was no denying the electricity present between the two of us.

"So what was the best thing you saw in Egypt?" I asked him, moving just marginally closer as other people walked around us following the church service.

"I was on a boat on the Nile," he started to explain when a voice right behind me interrupted.

"Okay, we only have a few minutes, so we need to hurry."

I had momentarily forgotten all about the dark-haired girl with the watches. She was still with me. This is *your* memory. So you need to grant me access."

"What?" I said, turning around to face her but still flipping glances over my shoulder at me and Mark, engrossed in conversation.

"No one can see us or interact with us just yet. I need to see your device real quick," she said, but I instinctively pulled it back.

"It's not a big deal," she said impatiently, crossing her arms in front of her. "I just need to hit a couple buttons so I can interact with Mark."

"Why? What are you going to do?" I demanded.

She sighed, giving me a look that resembled pity.

"Melanie," she said slowly, as if she were speaking to a rather stupid pet. "He is going to kill you and your baby. I have to take him out of the picture before that can happen. You *just* met the guy right now. If he dies, it will be a bad memory for you, but it won't be like suffering the loss of your husband. I'm being *kind*. But you have to grant me access. Do you touch him, do you know?"

"What?" My brain was working too slowly to process what was happening. There was a detached part of me that realized I should be demanding questions—questions about time travel, how what I was seeing was possible, even who the mysterious woman was. But all I could focus on was the past.

"Right now. In this memory. Do you touch him? Because as long as you make any skin-to-skin contact, I can interact with that person if you grant me access. Even touching his hand while exchanging phone numbers or something would be enough."

"Oh. Um...probably," I answered, but I was no longer looking at her. I was staring at me and Mark again, mesmerized. "So they can't see us?"

"Not unless you grant us—and specifically *me*—access," she said. I didn't need to look at her to perceive her mounting impatience. "And we only have *three* minutes in each memory, and I need time to take him out of the picture."

"How are you going to kill him?" I asked in a completely detached manner. I—the young me that is—was laughing at something Mark said, and his dimples were clearly showing as he smiled at my reaction.

"I have a gun. It'll cause a panic, but it'll be okay."

I nodded, not actually listening to her words.

"So grant me access."

"I...I can't."

"Melanie!" she shouted, and I spun to look at her. "We are almost out of time!"

"I…" I turned and looked at us again. I could practically feel my young heart beating. I had been exhilarated, and it was a wonder everyone in the room wasn't compelled to stop and stare at this conversation.

"Ugh. Fine," the woman said angrily. "We're almost out of time. Before we get sucked back to the present, I need you to think of a different memory with Mark, so I have time to get rid of him in another time. Quick. Think of something and touch the pad again."

I didn't want to leave us at the almost magical beginning of our relationship. But I touched the pad on the device.

I should have been freezing then, but I couldn't feel the air in the ice arena. "So we're not really here until I grant access?" I asked. I could feel the woman behind me, but my eyes remained focused on my younger self. I was wearing a university hoodie and screaming against the glass. Other people pushed in on the current me, I realized, but I passed right through them, as if they were ghosts.

Melanie didn't answer my question again, but instead said, "Why did you have to pick a super crowded place? We'll have to back up a little before you grant me access. Also, how do I get a clear shot at the ice—oh wait. I see. I can run around to the benches and shoot from there."

I looked at the ice. Mark was sporting our university colors— orange and black—from where he stood in goal, his goalie pads making him look huge. The other team was on a breakaway. Everyone around me screamed and cheered as Mark gloved the puck out of the air.

"Game's just about over anyway. This is going to be a really awkward one, but I can still try. Come over here and grant me access," Melanie said, directly behind me.

But I had my eyes on Mark. The ref dropped the puck for the faceoff. Only three seconds remained on the board. The other team didn't get another shot on Mark before the buzzer sounded and all of his teammates rushed Mark, jumping around him and congratulating each other. They had just won a huge game, making Mark the winningest goaltender in the school's history. I looked at myself. I was jumping up and down with everyone around me, hugging my college friend, Becca.

I had managed to forget about the woman behind me. "This one isn't going to work. Can you pick somewhere a little more secluded? I won't have time to get through these crowds."

I looked at Mark again, who was already skating toward the younger me at the glass. I've never forgotten that smile.

I thought of a similar look on his face, and I touched the watch screen again.

The setting was like something out of a movie. A lake, flowering bushes, butterflies everywhere. I still wasn't quite sure how we had stumbled upon this place—this little park that was a slice of paradise in the middle of crowded New Jersey. But stumbled upon it we had, and we had spent years picnicking there through college. College was ending the next day, though; and while we would both be going to a different college, still together, for graduate school, it certainly felt like the end of an era.

"I'm going to miss this place," my college self was saying, holding a sandwich and looking out at the lake. Had I been looking at him, I would have seen how Mark was practically shaking as he reached into the picnic basket behind me, pulling out a box.

He reached forward and rubbed my shoulder then. "Melanie," he said, and his voice shook just slightly. My younger self, my hair cut short then while I wore a picturesque, white, peasant-style skirt, turned to face him. He had the ring box behind his back. Mark's breath caught in his throat. "You—you are absolutely incredible. I love you so, so much."

"You seriously want me to kill him while he proposes to you?" a voice cut in. "Seriously? Well, your funeral. Grant me access."

"I..."

"Melanie, I want to spend the rest of my life with you," Mark said.

"Hello? Melanie?" the woman interrupted again. "Trying to save your life here."

I felt like I couldn't move. What she had been suggesting—killing Mark in order to save my life—was only just beginning to sink in. And yet I felt that there was no way that Mark would kill me. We loved each other, and I was seeing the beginnings of it so plainly before me!

"Ugh. Just please pick a different memory so that you can grant me access. Pick a boring memory. Maybe a boring dinner out with friends or something."

I closed my eyes to block out the light and touched the watch screen.   The wind howled in the dark outside, and even in the wood-paneled room, the lights were surprisingly dim.

"Well, thanks so much for having us over," I was saying, a fake smile plastered across my face.

"Of course!"

"Can we just say bye to Patty before we leave? Where is she?" I asked.

"Oh, she's probably in the next room with her little doodles," my old college friend, Becca, said, leading me, Mark, and her husband into the adjoining room.

"Goodbye, Patty," I said, bending down to the girl. "Oo. What are you working on?"

"A scientific design," the small child said.

"It's really very, very good!" I exclaimed, picking up a thick book from the desk and eyeing it momentarily. "What's your design for?"

"I'm not ready to say just yet," the girl calmly responded, looking up at my younger self, meeting my gaze directly. "You and Mr. Mark make designs for work, right?" Her eyes sparkled with life, even as her shoulders slumped.

"Yes. Mr. Mark's are for bridges and mine are for houses," I said kindly.

"Oh, Patty's always coming up with little pictures," Becca said abruptly. "Isn't it cute? We just have to remember to not waste too much paper when we're drawing them. Isn't that right, Patty?"

"Hey, rain let up," Mark cut in.

"Oo! Let's hurry before it gets heavy again," my younger self said. "Thanks again for having us!" I exclaimed as we practically ran to the front door. Mark held it open for me as I quickly said to Becca, "Hey. If you want, we could maybe take Patty to the museum near our house sometime. It's got dinosaurs and—"

"Oh, I wouldn't want Patty surrounded by all of *that*. I mean, it's not like dinosaurs actually existed."

"Gotcha. Well, thanks again for having us over, Becca. It was nice seeing you!" my other self finished, practically dashing through the front door. I naturally followed, only then remembering that the dark haired woman was presumably with me. She had been quiet, but making eye contact with me, she silently followed me out of the house.

I figured she would want full access to the memory, but I didn't offer it as I called over my shoulder, "How do I interact with the car without full access?"

She simply answered, "You can choose whether or not to interact with the physical items around you. So you can float through the doors, but still sit in the car seats."

I wanted to ask why she wasn't pressing for access, but instead I jumped into the backseat, the woman next to me. As soon as the car started, Mark turned to younger me. "Okay, it's not just me, right? They have gotten so *weird*."

"Yes!" my other self exclaimed, subconsciously spinning my engagement ring on my finger. "I mean, they live like hermits now," I said, referencing the woods around us. "And fine, I get not everyone wants to live in suburbia, but the whole sterilization thing when we went in the house!"

"Yes! That was super creepy. And the canned goods everywhere. If they were just into canning, fine. But they kept acting like it was the 1700s and referencing needing to cut more wood for the winter. And that comment about antibiotics!"

"And the dinosaur one at the end! And they're super weird with Patty, who is clearly intelligent. But they keep talking about her like she's messed up instead of gifted. Did you see that drawing she was working on?"

"Time's just about up. New memory please, and this time make it one that I can actually use," the woman said, surprising me with her voice. I was about to touch the screen when she added. "Make it simple on me and you. Choose the worst fight you've ever had. That way it won't be difficult for you to grant me access."

Mark and I didn't fight often, let alone scream at each other, so I knew exactly the moment to choose.

"I *needed* your help tonight!" Mark yelled. He had bags under his eyes, though he was dressed in a nice polo shirt and khakis. "You *knew* I was bringing Craig back with me, and I just asked you to clean up the downstairs, and you didn't. We looked like fucking trash! I've made things nice for you. Why couldn't you do the same for me?"

I was just shy of thirty, wearing bleach-stained sweatpants and no makeup. I barely reacted at all to Mark's tirade. I could feel the hurt all over again. I had let him down. Again. The dishes were piled high in the sink, there was a pile of dirty laundry obnoxiously close to the front door, and there were stacks of mail and forms I had half-heartedly been sorting spread out on the floor.

Mark had begged me to tidy things up for his boss, who was stopping over for dessert following their dinner to discuss one of Mark's ideas. Mark was always a partner in cleaning up the house, but he had been working long hours the past month, pouring his energy into this new project, and he had asked me to handle things a little more than usual to help him out.

I hadn't. In fact, I could barely find the strength to get out of bed those days. People at my own work had begun to notice my attitude change, and Mark was at his wit's end.

Mark yelled again. "Why can't you just act normal?" He kicked over the trash can, and both my younger and current selves jumped. Then he marched out the back door.

I already knew what I would do. I would collapse in a little ball on the floor and cry.

It was Mark who I wanted to see. I ran through the back door, following him, the woman hot on my heels.

"Okay. Perfect," she said the moment we were in my backyard. "Now grant me access."

Mark let out a guttural groan-yell, hands clenched at his sides. "God, why?" he yelled up into the night sky. He sat on the ground abruptly then and started to sob.

"Melanie, we're going to run out of time again!" the woman shouted.

I crouched down next to Mark, he was mumbling through his tears—whether to God or himself I couldn't tell. "I know she's depressed. And I want to have a baby too, but I'm not reacting like *that*. And I..." He heaved out a horrible sob. "I don't know what to do. I'm failing as a husband. And I have no idea what to do."

I reached slowly to put my hand on Mark's shoulder, only part of me realizing he wouldn't feel it. But the woman's voice stopped me. "Melanie! Give me access *now*!"

I stood up and faced her while Mark cried next to me.

"I can't," I said.

"He's going to kill you and your unborn child. Is that what you want?"

I looked back at Mark. "I don't believe he will."

"You saw the headline! What more proof do you want?" She stomped on the dirt. "If you don't do it for yourself, think about your baby. Your baby is going to die too!"

"If you kill Mark now my baby will never exist."

Melanie's eyes went wide for a second. "I have a way to prevent that, but we're running out of time. Is there a better moment to kill Mark before he kills you?" She looked at her watch. "Only thirty seconds left!"

I looked at her closely then—her long black hair, her piercing blue eye. Her heavy purse, which presumably concealed the gun she had referenced. She was tall—taller than me by at least a few inches.

"You said you're from the future, but you could make yourself appear to me and interact with me, so you must have touched me."

She exhaled loudly. "I delivered a package to you earlier, and brushed up against your hand when I did."

"But you're not my usual delivery person."   "Does it matter?"

"Did…did you know you might need to return to this day?"

"Pick a new memory!" she screamed, but it was too late.

I was standing back in the front room of my house, alone. There was a knock at the door. I looked out, and saw the woman standing there, but she looked different. She was holding a stack of papers in her hand, dressed in a casual skirt and shirt. Her hair was tied back from her face, and in that moment she looked vaguely familiar.

Indecision weighed on me, and before I could determine whether or not I wanted to open the door, she appeared behind me as well, looking as before with her hair blocking her face. "Don't answer that," she threatened quietly. "I have to figure out how to fix this now unless you're willing to cooperate. Would you like to read the articles?" she thrust them at me. I took them only for a second before allowing them to drop to the floor. "He shoots you and then buries you in the woods behind your house," the woman explained desperately.

"Mark doesn't even own a gun."

Her other self knocked on the door again.

"That's you, you know," I said to her.

The woman's eyes opened wide. Just then, I heard a car pull into the driveway. Mark was home.

The woman came to the window next to me. "I only have three minutes here," she said. "Please, if you value your life or the child's, take us to another memory so we can get rid of him."

"No," I said calmly. The other version of the woman, looking similar to the one in my house except for her hair, walked up to Mark and began conversing with him happily. "I'll risk it," I said, staring at my husband. "I love him, and he loves me."

The woman next to me reached into her purse then and pulled out the gun. She pointed it right at my head. "Take me to another memory. Now," she said through nearly closed lips.

Just then the front door flew open and Mark and the other version of the woman entered the house. "Melanie, this is Heather from the political—" he cut himself off. "You look terrified. What's wrong?"

"Don't let her shoot you yet!" the woman holding the gun screamed then. While her gun was pointed at me, her eyes were staring at the other version of herself.

"Don't ask. Just tackle her," I commanded Mark quickly.

I gave him credit, for he did exactly what I required of him, throwing himself at the woman in the skirt with the ponytail. "She has a gun on her!" I yelled. "Find it."

"Now take me to a different memory!" the woman not being tackled demanded.

There was chaos as the woman in front of me shouted and

Mark grappled with the other one. Mark was strong, though, and he quickly overpowered the one and pulled the gun out of the materials she had been holding. He held it out, pointed at her. "What the hell is going on, Mel?" he asked, breathing hard.

The two guns looked the same, one pointed at me from the time traveling woman, the other pointed from Mark toward the other woman, who had stood back up shakily.

"Call 9-1-1," I said, and Mark pulled out his phone.

"No!" the woman with the gun screamed. "I can still shoot you! Remember? I can interact with *you!*"

"But you don't want to because I'll be dead, and clearly you don't want me dead right now. Though you did," I said, inching myself slowly to stand next to Mark who was dialing 9-1-1.

"What?" he said to me.

"Ignore me. Just watch the girl and talk to the police." I started again, facing the woman with the gun, "So I'm guessing you came here to kill me. But something went wrong. And you needed to change it. What went wrong?"

Both women were shaking and staring at me, though I focused on the one with the gun still.

"I came to kill you," she said, the gun wobbling in her hand. "For how you left me to suffer."

"Let me have the gun," I said sternly to Mark, who did as he was told while he talked to the police. I kept it pointed at the woman in the skirt, just in case she had another weapon on her. "How did I leave you to suffer?" I asked the woman with the gun.

"You *saw* that my life was hell. My parents were idiots. I was a genius. You *saw* that when I was a child, and you did nothing to help me."

It clicked. "You're Patty."

"I go by Patricia now," she said, while the version of her in the skirt stared at me talking to seemingly empty space with her mouth open.

"Your parents seemed like backward people, but they were taking care of you. What was I supposed to do?"

"You and Mark were smart people. My parents kept me isolated for my entire childhood. It was only when I turned eighteen that I got leave. People found me. I helped create these time devices. But my entire childhood was hell. And you could have pulled me out of it."

"How? Your parents weren't abusing you or anything."

"But they were idiots! Horrible, annoying people. I *hated* my childhood. You could have come over, taken me out sometimes. Anything. Instead, you're going to give all of the experiences *I* wanted to this baby. You could have given them to *me*! But you did nothing!" She looked at the watch. There couldn't be much time left. Her mouth formed a grim line right before she determined, "I'm screwed either way now."

While she had never directed it away from me, the gun straightened ever so slightly in her hands. I acted before my brain could even register the danger. In an instant, I moved the gun toward the Patricia with the other gun and fired. Mark screamed and raced forward, but the bullet didn't go anywhere in the house. It stayed firmly lodged within Patricia as she fell to the floor. Blood began to seep through her shirt at her chest as her still body disappeared.

Mark was at my side, his eyes wide. He grabbed the gun from my unresisting hands and went back to holding it. My ears were ringing, but I finally began to hear sirens nearby.

I was barely processing the other version of Patricia near me when police barged into the house. Mark put the gun on the floor and we both backed away. As the police rushed toward all three of us, the other Patricia fell to the ground. There was yelling between police officers. I could barely take in what was going on, other than that the Patricia left with us, presumably from our time, had stopped breathing.

* * *

It must have been the middle of the night. Mark had been separated from me at the police station as we were questioned. It started with local police, then people in suits entered. Finally, different people in suits entered.

"Mrs. Brown," this last man said with a hint of warmth, coming forward and shaking my hand. "I am so, so sorry for what you've gone through today."

"It's—it's okay."

"Seriously. For *everything* you've gone through," he said, directing his eyes at me and lowering his head just slightly. He glanced at the door to the windowless room I had been sitting in. "We can speak freely in here," he said. "Our investigation took six months, but I believe I haven't made you wait too, too long I hope." It was then that I noticed the green watch he was wearing.

"I just spoke to your husband too. Explained everything. Even took him on a very brief trip to prove I wasn't...well, to prove I wasn't crazy. But I needed you both to know, it's over."

"It is?"

"Patricia Bowen was a designer on our team. An extraordinary mind. But, as you experienced, a bit...well. We looked into things. We don't blame you. What were you supposed to have done? But clearly Patricia blamed you for her lost childhood. We found diary entries wherein she described you two as being the only intellectual people she had ever come across in her childhood in person. I mean, she read extensively, but she was very sheltered. Her parents never let her leave the house. We thought she was excited to have a fresh start when she came to us, but apparently she had never let her past go. She was going to kill you today. She succeeded, as a matter of fact. Originally. Then she captured your husband, kept him in her basement for three months. She thought he made a good scapegoat—guilty husband who appeared to be on the run—and she kept him alive just to mess with him, to watch him live knowing you and your baby were dead. But what she didn't realize is that she was a suspect all that time. When law enforcement came for her, she knew she was caught. They would find your husband. They had more than enough evidence of her involvement. So she used one of the watches she created to go back in time, to try to kill him in a different time when she wouldn't be a suspect. How better to become *not* a suspect than to kill him in a time when she wasn't born yet, or at the very least was a young child? But that didn't work out. And when the original plan of killing you failed...well, she had a backup plan in place in case she were caught. She took the poison right before the police arrived."

I was struggling to take it all in.

"So it's over?"

"It's over." He smiled just slightly. "And from talking with the police, I'm guessing you probably killed the Patricia from the very near future. But being that she killed herself in an earlier version, that technically didn't come to pass. You're the only one with the memory of having killed her. So you don't have to worry about messy court proceedings. Plus, and I can't stress this enough, the official story is going to look *very* different from what actually happened."

❋ ❋ ❋

As soon as I was escorted out to the police station lobby, Mark ran up to me and gave me a hug. The man with the green watch followed us out, saying, "So, again, Mr. and Mrs. Brown, I'm very sorry you had to deal with that. That girl was very troubled, and you did a great job getting the gun from her. Why she targeted you, we'll never know, but at least it's all over."

"Yes. Thank you," Mark said as he walked me outside where a police officer drove us the short distance home.

As soon as we were in the privacy of our own home, Mark broke down crying, hugging me tight. "I can't believe any of this."

"I know," I said into his shoulder.

"So the shot you took?"

"Was at a slightly future version of Patricia," I said.

"And she time traveled around with you before I showed up, the guy told me."

"Yes."

"Trying to convince you to let her kill me."

"Yes."

"And you didn't."

"I was *never* going to. I love you."

He held me tighter. "I love you too."

Finally releasing me, I looked up into his eyes. "Where did you go? When you traveled with the man back in the police station."

"To the most life-changing moment of my life. The day I met you."

THE CHECK

By David Sangiao-Parga

After Abe mailed the check to Justin, he figured it was fifty-fifty whether the young man would darken his doorway again. So when he heard the growl of Justin's diesel F-350 long before it came into sight on the dusty road leading to Abe's farm, the only surprise was how long it had actually taken Justin to come out. The check was sent out over a week ago. Abe sighed and steeled himself, setting aside the rake he'd been using to clean up the hay stalls. Justin's truck came to a rough stop just outside the barn, kicking up a dust cloud with it.

Justin knew where Abe would be, of course. After three months on the farm, Justin knew Abe's daily routine inside and out.

Abe's hands already ached by the mid-morning, gnarled as they were with arthritis. He ran one of them shakily through the thinning strands of his hair, a habit he'd developed as a young man. Always best to look presentable as possible. A cold wind cut through his light sheepskin jacket, and he shook his head sadly. Winter came earlier to Nebraska every year.

"Hello, Justin," he called out as the man hopped out of the truck and slammed the door shut.

"Don't you hello me," he replied, jabbing an accusatory finger at Abe. "You cheated me!"

"What are you talking about?" Abe took a step back from Justin as he approached the old man.

"That check, that light fucking check. It's only for half of what you said you'd pay me!"

"Justin, I told you already in the letter I sent," Abe said, keeping a cautious distance. "I said I might not have enough on hand to pay it all at once."

"No, that ain't how this works. I did an honest summer's work for ya, and I need that money now."

"I don't have it all yet," Abe said. "Give me a few more weeks."

"I don't got a few more weeks!" Justin yelled. "I gotta be moved out in two days, and I need that money for the road." That was a surprise. Abe had just helped Justin find that apartment less than a month ago. If he was already leaving, and needing cash, that meant he was desperate.

"Justin, your personal problems aren't mine. I told you that weeks ago."

Abe felt his heartbeat quicken just a bit as he looked at Justin. Was he using again already? It was hard to tell. Abe had never touched any of that stuff, not even during his tours overseas. He'd been able to keep Justin mostly clean over the summer, offering him room and board instead of a weekly wage. It was easier to manage that way. Subsidies weren't going as far as they used to anymore.

Justin stepped forward, his eyes blazing. He was close enough now that Abe could smell the whiskey on the boy's breath. "You got money stashed away, I know you do." He looked around furtively, scanning the driveway leading up to the house. "Where's Mary?"

"She's gone to town with some friends. Gonna have lunch, maybe play some euchre later, I think. Ladies day on the town, I suppose." Abe was thankful for the good fortune that Justin had stopped by on a day his wife was out until after dark.

"Good," Justin said. He pointed with his chin towards the house. "Let's go."

"Are you really planning to rob me?" Abe asked.

"It's not robbing if I'm takin' what's owed, now is it?" He pushed Abe hard in the chest, almost hard enough to knock the older man over. "Move it."

Slowly, Abe turned and walked towards the house in his steady, unhurried way. "And if I don't have the money you want?"

"Then we're gonna have to move on to Plan B," Justin said. Abe didn't move. Justin narrowed his eyes and motioned towards the house again.

"What're you waiting for?" he asked.

"Have you thought this through?" Abe responded. He went on without waiting for a reply. "No, I don't think you have. How far do you believe you'll get? Do you really think I won't report this?"

"I think," Justin said, pulling an old pistol out of his jacket pocket, "that for now you just need to worry about the next ten minutes."

It was far from the first time Abe had a gun pointed at him, but it never failed to get his blood pumping. The gun changed everything. Abe's lips tightened into a thin line, and his hands shook. He wondered if Justin noticed.

As they walked to the house, Abe tried to reason with Justin. "I don't know why you're doing this. If you needed help, I've always been happy to give it."

"Aw gee, thanks Dad," Justin said. Abe could practically hear the sneer. "You think just cause I worked for you a few months, that means anything?" He chuckled humorlessly. "Like it's gonna make us family or some shit? Boy, you're a real softie, Abe."

They marched up the steps of the porch and reached the front door. Instead of reaching for the doorknob, Abe began rooting in his pockets.

"What are you doing?" Justin asked.

"Just need to get my keys," Abe said. "Mary's been insisting I keep the door locked when no one's in the house." He curled his fist inside the pocket and made a show of struggling to pull it out. "Did you cash that check I sent you, at least?" Abe asked.

"Yeah, just before I came here," Justin said.

"On a Sunday?"

"From my phone, old man. Get with the times. I'll have the money first thing tomorrow."

"Oh good," Abe replied, and turned on Justin with a pocket knife clenched in his hand, jamming it in the young man's jugular with well-practiced effortlessness. Justin gaped wide-eyed as he staggered and fell to the ground, blood pooling on the porch underneath him. Abe hummed and opened the door, dragging Justin's body inside and down the stairs into the basement.

About an hour later, Abe was looking at his handiwork. Justin had been lean and toned from a summer of work, and Abe had fed him well. The meat was marbled evenly. Thankfully, there was a rendering plant about five miles south. Once he mixed the offal with whatever scraps were left from the livestock, no one would be the wiser. He took the check, the one Justin had lost his life over, and crumpled it in his hands, stuffing it deep into his coat. He chided himself for not getting the paper shredder his wife had suggested purchasing last year.

Above him, he heard the distinct sound of his wife's feet as she walked up the porch steps. He swore, a habit he rarely indulged these days, as he remembered the bloody smears on the deck and across the hardwood floors. He knew he'd forgotten something. As Mary came down the basement steps, Abe turned to her with a bloody knife in his hand. His eyes were wide with fear.

"Oh my god, Abe!" she cried. Abe stammered, at a loss for words. She narrowed her eyes. "If you expect me to clean up that porch for you, you have another thing coming."

"I'm sorry about that. Thought I'd be all done before you got home."

"No, Sue Ellen had an emergency. No euchre today." She sighed and surveyed the basement. "Is that Justin?"

"It is," Abe said with some hesitation.

"Really, hon," Mary said, "If you can't follow the rules, you're going to have to stop eating people."

"Don't worry," Abe said. "Our alibi's solid. He cashed the check I sent. Why would he come back here?"

Mary tightened her lips and looked around the basement. "I'll go ahead and put some peroxide and bleach on the porch, but I think you're still going to have to paint it."

"Ayup. I was planning to do that anyway." He hoisted a piece of meat wrapped in butcher paper and twine. "What do you think? Dinner?"

"I'll get the broiler pan out," Mary said. She smiled and gave Abe a kiss on the cheek. As she turned to leave, Abe saw he'd left a smear of blood on her face. He whistled the Andy Griffith tune while he followed her up the stairs.

ROMANCE THROUGH REVISION

By Ellen Parry Lewis

Every time I receive one of your letters, I fall more in love with you.

I keep that part of a letter framed in my office, a reminder of how I was put on this journey three years ago.

I was sitting in my nana's attic, helping my mom go through all of her things in the days following the funeral. I had thought my mom would have been eager to go through every single item, reminiscing about her childhood. But I ended up being the one who got stuck reading old papers and looking at creased photographs. There were just so many stories in that old attic. Old notes from friends and elementary school poems. A poorly sketched tyrannosaurus rex and a snapshot of my grandmother at the beach with poofy, curled hair.

But when I picked up that small box labelled "Mom and Dad," I knew I had something special. It was filled with letters, crumpled, stained, yellowed, and folded. The stamps alone probably would have been enough to spark my imagination, but when I *opened* the letters, the story practically manifested itself.

My great-grandparents, who had lived on the same street growing up, had begun exchanging letters during the war. The letters began casually friendly, my great-grandmother telling my great-grandfather about what was happening at home, him telling her about his travels. But they quickly grew deeper, more poetic, with more secrets laid openly, invitingly before the other.

I had just finished my MFA program, and the need to put this romance into book form was practically tangible, like a current moving through my nana's dim attic.

I started as soon as I got back to my apartment that night. And I managed to tease out of those brittle, almost crusty letters the life that was hidden within the ink.

I never met my great-grandparents, but they are now more real to me than some of my friends. I know the exact way they smile as they hold the letters; the thoughts that run through my great-grandfather's head as he believes he's about to die; the way my great-grandmother stares at the moon on a cold night in December, wondering if the moon looks the same overseas. I see them as they dance for the first time at a town fair after his return, her head on his shoulder; the way they hold hands and look at the moon, together now.

And then, a couple weeks ago, I got the long-awaited news. A small publishing company in Philadelphia wanted to publish the resultant novel. I was actually going to be an author. The dream was real.

I stare at the letter in my office for another second, and then open my email. I immediately spot a message from my new publisher through the junk mail and open it:

Dear Brian Cresswald,

I'm Lauren Caplan, and I am very excited to work with you as your editor on your book.

Crap. The editor. The part I was dreading is finally upon me. I *know* I'm supposed to like the idea of an editor. A forced willingness for deep revision was practically beaten into me in college. And yet I *still* resist it. After all, isn't an editor's job to take your prose, your story, your soul on paper, and stomp on it until it is something *marketable*?

I take a deep breath and hold it for a moment, forcing myself to move on:

I am very excited to take on your project. While the idea of falling in love through letters is nothing new—oh, you're already trashing my very idea—*your language was fresh and the story timelessly romantic.* Sure, flatter me before you tear me apart.

I'm sharing a document with you now that I will be editing as I go. I will reach out to you when I specifically want you to look at something, but you can always check on my progress in the interim. I wanted to let you know that I work as hard as I can to keep my authors' voices authentically theirs. Well, that sounds impossible. *Additionally, I frequently edit through the use of questions*—does she not know what she's doing?—*and also through sharing my emotions.* This isn't a free counseling session, lady. *I find that doing this sometimes gives you insight into your potential readers' thoughts and experiences while reading your book.*

I'm looking forward to working with you.

> *Lauren*

Whatever. I guess I'll look at her edits, and ready myself to fight for my book...as long as I don't lose the publishing deal in the process.

I already hate this.

* * *

Two weeks pass before I gather the courage to open the document and take a peek at it. I had expected to see it already riddled with strikethroughs and additions, but I instead find marginal comments here and there.

"I love the imagery here with the moon like a mirror," I read aloud before muttering, "Trying to make me let down my guard."

I scan a couple more and find positive comments until I get to page four. "Aha!" I say to myself as I start reading: *I was confused here. Why does Esther tell Robert she is looking forward to the dance next week if she's actually dreading it?*

"Ugh…because she's trying to make herself sound happier than she really is," I say to my computer screen. I respond that way to her comment and log off. One edit is a good enough start. I'll come back to it later.

* * *

"Later" only proves to be an hour. The editor, Lauren, has already responded, and I find that she is actively engaged in leaving more comments on my manuscript.

But why *is she trying to make herself sound happier? After all, she starts off the letter trying to make herself seem appropriately bored and sad, so as to not upset Robert with him being in danger overseas,* she had responded.

I give in and read over the preceding page. Sure enough, Esther does play back and forth between those emotions a little haphazardly. It makes sense in my head, but I never really dive into those seemingly opposite goals. I am actually a bit mad at Lauren as I start typing and tweaking. But as I finish, I see her cursor hovering near mine, and a comment left nearly the minute I have finished adding some words.

Much clearer, Lauren writes. *I now see the tear here, and how she is trying to take his mind off of the war while also not making him long too much for home so soon.*

"Fine. You got one, Lauren," I mumble half-heartedly, and I move on to another one of her comments.

I am so frustrated for Robert here! she has written, referencing a spot where Robert is about to be separated from a couple of soldiers for whom he has no respect.

Frustrated? Why on earth would she feel frustrated? I type as much, and am actually relieved to see her answer my question almost right away: *Because now Robert will never get the chance to show them he's a better person than they think!*

"But they don't matter! They're nobodies," I respond.

Haha! Well, I suppose you're a more confident person than I am then.

Confident? What do I have to be confident about compared to Lauren? I'm just getting my first book published. She already has a job as an editor at a publishing company. A small publishing company, but still. I'm in my late twenties simply working a boring job at a book store while I write my own stuff, hoping to keep the momentum going after this first book.

I tap my fingers on my desk for a minute, mulling over my thoughts. Finally, curiosity overcomes me and I go on the publisher's website and click on the "Editors" tab. There aren't many listed, and I quickly find Lauren Caplan. Upon seeing her, I'm even more confused as to what she wouldn't be confident about! She has to be about my age, short wavy hair, almost black, with cool cat eye glasses not most women could pull off. But she does. She looks so purely awesome with her glasses and slightly asymmetrical smile, like she looks like she gets the inside joke and you don't. Her arms are crossed in front of her, and although the picture stops before her legs, you can tell from the way her shoulders are squared to the camera and her hips are just slightly angled that she's got some spunk in her.

I go back to my book now, the image of Lauren Caplan in my mind as I read her next comment.

Okay, I'm afraid here. I can see Robert getting sent home in pretty bad shape, even if he's not dead.

I laugh a little aloud. "Good. You're supposed to be afraid," I type.

I figured as much, she responds. *But that doesn't mean I have to like it. Well, I like it from a plot standpoint, but I don't like it, if you know what I mean.*

I smile. I do know what she means.

Her next two suggestions are about drawing out the imagery I started to dabble in. *You mention the feel of the grass, but I can't quite see your character's thoughts. And then you almost connect this to Robert sitting on the grass in the next scene, but it falls just short of connecting the two of them.*

I sit for a moment, practically stunned. I realize then that that's the way my mind had been working, but it must have gotten stuck or distracted by the words somewhere in between. I fix it, connect Esther's hand to Robert's.

The result of this added material is magic, Lauren writes, and I agree.

There is magic there, and Lauren helped me see it.

❋ ❋ ❋

A week into this, and I feel like I know Lauren almost as much as I know Esther and Robert. I know what makes her feel sad and frustrated, happy and excited, scared and distressed.

She must sense it, though, too, because recently she told me to change a couple of things back to the way I had them before I edited them preemptively. "But I know this scene was going to bother you," I insist.

That's true. But I'm not going to be your only reader, and there is nothing at all wrong with the way you had it. It was good for your story.

But I want to make Lauren happy, write a book that she connects with as deeply as the sections where we both feel the magic together. But she insists that there is magic in some places, even if it's not what *she* would have written. Because it's what *I* wrote.

I feel seen.

And when I look at the letter on my desk, I edit it quite simply in my mind:

Every time I receive one of your revisions, I fall more in love with you.

* * *

Hi Brian,

Next week our publishing company is going to be at a book festival in New Jersey, I believe only a half an hour or so from where you're located. Obviously your book isn't out yet, but would you like to come anyway? I can print up some fliers about your soon-to-be-released book, and you can talk with people about it, give them some preorder information? I'd love to meet you in person!

Lauren

I read the email through twice.

Yes, I will go to the book festival.

* * *

The sky is bright and filled with marshmallow clouds as I walk through the closed-off street. Vendors are almost done laying out stacks of books, and open-sided tents are adorned with company and author banners. Some tables are already finished, and the occasional festival-goer has already entered the street and is browsing and talking to eager authors with painted-on smiles.

I have made it. I belong here.

I look down the road where I was informed my publisher would be located. I see my publisher's tent, a large banner at the top, but more importantly, beneath that, I see Lauren.

So it wasn't an old photograph. She's still just as young and just as impressive. As I walk closer, her eyes—I couldn't tell in the photograph if they were green or brown, but I see now they are brown—lock on mine. I smile. "Lauren?" I say hesitantly.

She smiles her crooked smile at me. "Yes. Are you Brian by any chance?"

"Yes," I say, unexpected relief washing over me at having been identified. "I'm surprised you recognized me only from that bio pic I sent you. My hair looks much darker in that photo than in real life."

"Yes, you are blonder in real life. But you've got the same bright blue eyes!" she says happily, and I grin on the inside. "I mean, are those colored contacts?"

"No. All me."

"Well, you're lucky," she says, turning and grabbing a stack of papers as she speaks. "A lot of people would kill for eyes that color," she finishes, handing me the papers. "These are for you to hand out to people as they come by."

I look at the flier, a colorful thing full of information and praise for my book. "Thanks for doing this for me, and inviting me to the event."

"Of course! We love it when our authors are able to participate in things like this. It's nice that you're so close to us," she says, and then she looks up as a man approaches our table. He looks maybe thirty, a rather muscular build in contrast to what I try to tell myself is my "scholarly body." His dark hair is perfect, his t-shirt tight, and he walks right up to Lauren.

I wait for her to say hello, introduce herself, but he leans over the table and gives her a familiar kiss right on her perfectly asymmetrical lips.

"Hey. You got here earlier than you thought you would," she says to him.

"Yeah, well, we finished early and I was able to come right here," the man says with a casual shrug of his shoulders, his eyes on Lauren.

She turns to me then, "Brian, this is my husband, Jeff."

"Oh? Nice to meet you," I say, extending a limp hand to him, which he takes firmly.

"Brian Cresswald?" Jeff asks, his voice deep and friendly. "Lauren's told me all about your book. She loves it. Apparently you know how to write quite the romance."

I laugh without life. "Yeah, well, I guess I'm just a hopeless romantic."

"You're preaching to the choir," Lauren says with a smile. "When I first met Jeff, we used to send each other emails. You see, I left right afterwards to study abroad for a semester. One of the first things we ever talked about is how we're both hopeless romantics. And it really was true." Her smile at him kills me a little bit.

"Are...are you an editor too?" I ask, even though my question is unlikely at best. He's too good-looking—probably a high school gym teacher or something.

"I'm a marriage counselor actually," he says, and I think I hate this man. No one should be that handsome *and* academic.

"So as I was walking here, I noticed that the ice cream cart just opened up, and I saw they have some sort of fudge swirl," Jeff says with a knowing wink at Lauren.

"Yes!" she says, standing up and moving around from behind the table. "Brian, feel free to take a seat and start talking to people. I'll be back in just a minute. Can I get you anything?"

"Oh, no thanks. I'm good," I say with a wave of my hand and what I hope is a smile. I sink into a chair as Lauren laces her fingers through Jeff's and they walk off together.

I stare blankly at the table in front of me. I realize then how much I had built up my idea of Lauren. How I thought we were, in some strange way, falling in love through our words— through her revisions that showed me her emotions, thoughts, and fears. But she had already used her writing to fall in love with somebody else.

I take a deep breath.

"Are you Brian Cresswald?" a voice nearby asks.

"Huh?" I look up dumbly. A woman is there, petite in every way except for her saucer-sized dark eyes with long lashes. She is holding one of the fliers about my book. "Oh, yeah. I'm Brian," I answer.

"Your book sounds really interesting. And it says here it's inspired by a true story?"

"Yeah," I say. "My great-grandparents' letters to each other."

She nods as if she knows all about it. "I feel like those sorts of romantic gestures don't happen anymore, you know? Maybe that's why I've given up entirely and write about dragons." She lets out a single-breath laugh and smiles at me directly.

"You're an author here?" I ask.

She nods her head. "Three tables down."

"And you write fantasy?"

She nods again. "Yes. Though I doubt I have your talent for prose," she says, fingering a spot on the flier, which I now see contains a blurb about my supposedly masterful use of language.

"Oh, I don't know," I say. "Dragons have the potential to be beautiful, I'd imagine, demanding some fairly intense descriptions."

She tilts her head to the side, her long, brown hair spilling over her shoulder. "I'll have to send you some snippets, see what you think."

I smile. "I'd like that."

"Here's my email," she says, scribbling on the corner of my flier and tearing it off for me. "Send me a message. I'll share my dragon descriptions with you, and you can send me something of yours."

"I will."

CHASING STARS

By J.M. Robison

Chapter One

Jessica pressed her palm against the glass, heat fogging around her hand. Cold. Wet. *Rain* pattered outside, slicking the rails and swirling across hot platforms. She might spend her entire lunch break watching it, neglecting her tea and croissant, but she didn't know when she'd see rain again.

It appeared God didn't think a city like Salt Lake needed rain, not when they paved over grass and uprooted trees to build yet more pomp and power.

After a blissful moment, the rain stopped. As if her hand had reached through the glass and touched the rain, she pressed her fingertips against her cheek, taking a second to selfishly love something man did not create—a rare occurrence, one that she barely knew herself as current science admitted there were still things man could neither stop nor duplicate. Rain reminded her of rebellion, falling without bias on the heads of those who raged they could not control it.

Her hand warmed again as she resumed sipping her tea. Her earcuff announcing the time, she grabbed her purse and left the table. The café doors opened with a whoosh and she stepped out, pressing her ring against the electronic pad beside the door. The device dinged once. Signal received.

Tucking her skirt beneath her, she sat on the bench—already dry—and said, "WebNet, play the latest social posts," to her earcuff. Her transportation took long enough that she was able to catch up on her friends' latest updates and a small snatch of news before the Railed Transport Pod glided to a transitionless halt on the rails in front of her. She slid inside the RTP, the robotic door lowering on its own. "Where is it you want to go?" the computer asked.

"Intellecta, level 1375."

A baby could sleep with how quiet and seamless the magnetized RTPs glided across the rails. It turned ninety degrees left before it shot straight up, flawlessly communicating with the rail and other RTPs to navigate the web spun around buildings and reaching to lower levels. The purring atmosphere inside the RTP eased her into a sense of solitude as if she were the only one out today despite thousands upon thousands of RTPs rising, diving, spiraling left and right all around her. Like a string of flowing pearls hanging on the city's neck.

Her RTP stopped at the platform outside Intellecta and the door opened.

Preoccupied with the copy she was expected to propose after lunch, she stepped out without her purse.

The RTP chirped. "Please remove your belongings."

"Oh, sorry," she said, even though computers had no feelings. At least not yet. Apparently, Intellecta tinkered in that, too. She grabbed her purse and went through two automatic doors.

She walked into her office, everything powering on to welcome her back. Hoping her excursion outside cleared her mental palate, she keyed up her recorder.

"Trust your life. Trust science," her recorded voice said.

"Give it one star," she said to the computer to score the line.

"Last phrase, three stars," answered a robotic voice.

Every day Jessica listened, scoring and un-scoring. This was her last chance to listen to her phrases before she had to present her final, best self-scored phrase to be used by Intellecta's marketing team.

"When your heart stops, let us keep it going."

Take away a star.

"Last phrase, one score. Next phrase: Let Intellecta spark your life."

Add one star.

Three more phrases and Jessica paused the recorder. She'd heard them many times already, so of course they sounded tired. Now was not the time to come up with a brand new phrase without it being vetted through her usual scoring method. But...

"Recorder, start new."

"Begin new."

She chewed on the tip of her finger. "Life is your choice. Recorder, stop."

"Recording has stopped. Replay?"

"Yes."

Excitement warmed her as she listened to her new recording. The rain made her think of it, how it chose to live despite all the odds, despite science's grudge against its independent existence. The Intella-heart could keep people alive, making their life*their* choice not governed by the inescapability of death.

Her heart stomped in her chest. She wanted to use it. Place it as her number one. But would it sound as good tomorrow? Hold its zeal as it blasted through everyone's earcuff and inside every RTP next week?

The rain dared fall upon Intellecta today. She would dare too. Excited, she gave the phrase six stars and told the recorder to gather her next top two. With more spring in her high heels, she walked to the conference room, taking a detour into the bathroom to touch up her hair and makeup.

Diedra and Angela entered the bathroom a moment after, Diedra anchoring herself in front of the mirror in a similar fashion to Jessica, pulling a black tube out of her purse and swiping it at her thick upper lashes.

"How would *you* decide then?" Diedra asked the redhead leaning against the wall next to her, continuing whatever conversation they had been engaged in before the bathroom.

"Whoever contributes to society the most."

"Angie, *everyone* contributes to society. There are very few who don't, and taking them out wouldn't even be half a percent of the total population." Diedra pulled out lipstick next and dragged it against her lips as Angela pushed off the wall with a certain warmth toward the subject.

"I said the *most* contribution."

"Well, neither you nor I fall into *that* category when compared to, like, the CEO of Intellecta. So, according to you, we'd both die." Angela's gaze roved around the room, across the sinks to where Jessica stood on the opposite end, dabbing the finishing touches of her foundation to her forehead. "How would *you* govern population control, Jessica?"

"Uh…" A victim of time and place, she searched in vain for an opinion on this controversial subject to give to this pair. "I chose to be a copywriter. Not a judge."

"It's people like you, Jessica, who feed into the problem. The city can't go up any higher because there isn't enough oxygen, and if people are living longer and dying less, we're going to run out of resources and we will *all* die. And Intellecta has the gall to create a heart to make you live even *longer*."

Jessica mumbled for a response, but Diedra snapped her powder case closed and walked out of the bathroom, Angela following. Despite her detour, Jessica made it to the conference room much too early. She sat on the couch, rubbing sweaty palms against her skirt.

Jephron entered the conference room. He sat at the table and turned to her. "Got us a winner, Jessica?"

Too nervous for words, she nodded.

"One that will convince these RTP-sitters to finally stop off at Intellecta's porch?"

"No fancy tagline is going to do that, Jephron." She lowered her eyelashes. "That's *your* job."

"Oh." He tucked into his chair as if embarrassed. "Someone should have told me then. Guess we're going to lose. Unless, of course, you save the day by producing an amazing tagline that will sway nations to our cause like an ancient battle cry."

She giggled. "That's *exactly* what it's going to do."

"Good girl. I knew there was a reason why Haverick wanted to keep you around."

Where Jephron's easy humor loosened her nerves, hearing her boss's name tightened them again.

Haverick Edelson, CEO of Intellecta, judge, jury, and executioner of his business, he easily claimed a seat next to the top five most powerful people in Salt Lake, staring the overpopulation controversy in the eye by creating the Intella-heart, which would extend the lifespan of anyone by at least twenty years.

That is, if anyone would buy it. Hell, take it for free.

As if her thoughts had summoned him, the man in charge of her dreams coming true entered the conference room. Good thing they were all going to listen to her recordings and not have her say them out loud. Her nerves would prevent her from remembering any of her taglines despite having worked on them for a month. She might literally die from anxiety right now.

Haverick sat at the head of the table. Jessica couldn't help but think that success only touched larger men. Not fat men. Just... large, as if they physically consumed their success, which added length to their bones and muscle to their shoulders. Or they bulked up by wrestling with all their skinny competition.

He intimidated Jessica, even though he smiled and said nice words to her whenever they landed in the same break room.

Arriving at the last minute, in walked Jephron's marketing partner and three publicists. More or less settled in their chairs, Haverick stood, splaying thick palms on the smooth table.

"Before Jessica proceeds with her presentation, I want everyone to put this in their mind first: which tagline is going to convince the undecided to finally proceed?"

"Before we can decide on a tagline," spoke one of the marketers, "we first need to know why people are resistant to replacing their heart with a machine."

"People are afraid the operation will kill them," a publicist offered. Others chimed in with: "The public thinks it won't work," "Can it be hacked?"

Haverick looked around the room, but no one offered anything further. "Now let's list the reasons why people *should* get the Intella-heart. "It will stop diseases before they start."

"Will never give you a heart attack."

"Will keep proper levels of all essential nutrients and will regulate cholesterol. If anything kills you, it won't be because of poor health." They listed several more benefits, but Jessica barely heard them over the roar in her ears as the moment approached when they would choose one of her taglines.

"All right." Haverick spun in his chair and smiled at her. "With those thoughts in mind, Jessica, give us your best phrases that will link both those thoughts together."

In a quiet tone, she synced her recorder to the one in the room and told it to play.

Everyone listened intently to all three, Jessica roiling with nerves over what they would think about the one she created an hour ago. "Everyone, cast your votes." Haverick's heavy gaze linked with each of theirs in turn. "Raise your hand for, *life is your choice.*" No one moved.

Embarrassment flushed her cheeks. She should have waited a day to hear it one more time. She would never make *that* mistake again. She looked out the window, but all remnants of the rain had vanished. A yearning filled her, but she could not place what for.

"Raise your hand for, *trust your life, trust science.*"

Everyone raised their hand.

"There we have it." Haverick grinned at her. "Thank you, Jessica, for such a wonderful tagline." He touched his earcuff and spoke some randomized passwords, finishing with, "add 300 dollars to Jessica Halwater's account, ID number 6756233."

Jessica's earcuff chimed with a quiet message saying the money had been deposited. "Thank you, Haverick."

He turned to his staff. "Jephron, I want you to push this tagline out immediately to all your marketing outlets. We've got thousands on the verge of consideration for the Intella-heart. Pending your marketing plan works the way you promised it would, payout will be astronomical. To everyone in this room, if we can get even a thousand to install the heart, you will all receive a very *generous* bonus."

Jessica perked up on the edge of the couch. Everyone else leaned toward Haverick as if he held the bonus in his hand.

"Good luck to all of you. You are dismissed."

Jessica stood on shaky knees. Her tagline was really just that pop of color to the actual marketing plan, much like a single cherry topped on a white-frosting cake.

She listened to the gentle murmurs of everyone else as they pushed back chairs.

"Too bad we don't have Ayden around to give us a product review," the blond publicist said.

"Too bad," grumbled her partner. "We'd already have that bonus by now." *Ayden.* Patient zero. Dying of lung cancer. In a coma. His parents acting as his legal guardians made the decision to accept Intellecta's free offer to remove his heart and replace it with the Intella-heart. The heart had just completed its final testing phase and now needed a human to try it on. With the Intella-heart plugged into Ayden's chest, the boy woke up. Cured.

The heart uses top secret Intellecta science to cure *all* ailments—and prevent future ones—from aggressive cancers to acne, by regulating blood flow, dictated by the heart. Once the doctor verified Ayden's cancer had been cured, his parents rejoiced, Intellecta cheered.

Ayden ran away.

Jessica had been woken out of a dead sleep by an emergency broadcast shrilling across her earcuff, giving a rapid description of the boy across the entire network. Intellecta offered a tremendous reward for his return. Despite his picture shared around the media that entire first year, no one found him. Three years later, he'd nearly become a myth. His parents, always ashen-faced when asked if they had any idea, would mutely shake their heads, provide stilted answers, and flee the ravenous media. Grief did weird things to people.

Intellecta had all the documentation from the doctor to prove his cancer was cured, but with his disappearance, people immediately discounted the Intella-heart.

"Why did he run away," they all asked, "if your product was so good? Unless, of course, it *killed* him."

Ayden's parents didn't have the answer. Nor Intellecta. They'd been fighting public opinion ever since.

"Unnatural," the public muttered.

"How does it work?" others asked.

But Intellecta would not advertise the one magic element geared to making the heart function, because they didn't want to advertise their secrets to Loginetics, their competitor in Las Vegas. So people didn't trust it. And might not if Ayden did not return. It had taken Intellecta the last year aggressively marketing the heart to even get people considering it. Haverick believed a single, good marketing campaign would finally tip them over the edge to where they would march into Intellecta already undressing for surgery.

Jephron sidled up next to Jessica as she left the room. "I'm counting on you for that bonus," he said. "Your tagline better make me thousands."

"You're the one who voted on it. So, really, if it fails, then it will be *your* fault. Not to mention that it's *your* marketing plan that will make or break the lure of the Intella-heart. In comparison, my tagline has nothing to do with it. I'm going to go preorder a Senicci dress, so if I don't get that bonus *because of you*, then I'm going to sit outside your office and cry until you sell everything you own to pay for that dress."

"Sounds like a new identity in the near future for me then." He turned down the hallway. "See you later, Jess."

Jessica's summoned RTP arrived with a smooth rise of its door. She slid inside mid-chew on her donut pillaged from the meeting.

"Where is it you want to go?" asked the computer.

"Level twelve–" she inhaled powdered sugar from her pastry and coughed, "–thirty!" she wheezed, coughing more as the door closed and the RTP moved.

The news stream spun up inside the RTP, and Jessica listened to Jephron's grand marketing advertisement about the heart for the first time. Despite their teasing, it impressed her to the point of considering the heart for herself in the future.

"Well done," she whispered to the space around her.

She sat back and opened her earcuff, a stream of updates filling her ear: Cassandra got her promotion. Michael burnt his toast. Logan ranted about President Frodshore with the meme, "The president is a *Frod*."

Hendrix was pouring out his unpopular opinion about population control when Jessica realized the RTP hadn't stopped when it certainly should have.

The window showed a darkening city. Not because it was even close to dark, which still made no difference because the city lights kept the entire sky bright as day no matter the time, but because she was descending lower than she wanted.

Her gaze shot up to the screen on the console where numbers flickered in descending order.

Fifty-three...fifty-two...fifty-one...

"No! RTP, STOP!"

"Stopping without a platform is dangerous and will not be acknowledged."

"Stop at the next platform!"

"Acknowledged."

The RTP slowed, stopping at platform forty-six.

The door opened. "Please remove your belongings."

"No! No! take me to level 1230!"

"Please remove your belongings."

"Stupid computer!" Jessica kicked the console, her high heel punching a dent into the soft Arboform.

A lonely light illuminated the platform. Blackness shrouded all else beyond.

Anxiety ratcheted her heart rate. The RTP had stopped damn near the *ground*. Salt Lake continuing to grow upward, ancient buildings layered over myth, past layered over ancient, new layered over past, and future endeavors topped them all three miles at the top. No city lights bled down this far. The only reason a bulb hovered above this platform was because state mandate decreed every platform would be lit. Even at ground zero, though Jessica doubted a human had set foot on the dirt in nine hundred years. Even Understreet degenerates didn't venture below level one hundred. Ghosts and witchcraft, they said.

"Please remove your belongings," the RTP reminded in an infinitely patient voice.

Because of the massive amount of traffic in Salt Lake, you owned your wrong directions, so to get the RTP to take you to the right platform, you had to get out and rekey it. Problem though, is once the pressure sensors on the seat relax, the door closes, and the RTP leaves.

So the only way to get out of this horrid, lost, cold, abandoned platform was to get out and rekey. Problem: she couldn't see the keypad normally illuminated by a tiny green light.

She doubted maintenance dropped below level 300. Likely a keypad had not even been installed this close to the ground, not with houses and businesses all much higher up where people actually *went*. She'd have to find a staircase and walk up three miles. She had no food or water. The wireless signal didn't reach down this far, so she couldn't even call for help over the WebNet.

She sobbed, fear hurting her bones, the RTP reminding her over and over to remove her belongings. She couldn't even ask her earcuff for help with information on how to survive on the ground. After exploring all her options with ragged twists on her skirt, she came to the horrid conclusion she would *have* to get out if she were going to get back in.

She had to find the keypad. Sloppy maintenance on a level as ancient as the Middle Ages probably put the pad around the corner where she couldn't see the green light. She asked her earcuff one more time for help, but it remained silent. Like the rest of the world immediately around her.

She stepped out. The door closed. The RTP rose upward on the rail. Too terrified to move, she stood on the platform under the light of a single bulb.

Finally, some reason pushing and scratching to the forefront of her brain told her the sooner she found the keypad, the sooner she could leave.

Drawing in a shuddering breath, she turned and stepped toward the concrete wall. She walked to the edge of the light, searching the darkness. No green light.

A rattle of metal somewhere beyond made her scream and scuttle directly beneath the light bulb. "Stay back," her shaky voice barely whispered.

More noise. Closer this time.

Her whisper matured into a scream. "Get away from me!"

Steady steps now, thumping along a ramp arching out into the darkness. She couldn't see beyond the light.

Her heart seized as a body stepped out of the darkness.

Death-white skin and black holes for eyes.

She couldn't scream because she couldn't breathe.

A ghost.

This is where she would literally die.

She passed out instead.

Chapter Two

"Hey." Someone tapped her cheek. "Hey."

She blinked and looked up into the blinding light of the single bulb. And a face. A perfectly normal, human face. A young man, maybe nineteen or twenty. Blond hair. Blue eyes.

"You okay?" he asked.

He leaned back as she sat up. She held her head, touching the lump from where she must have struck it when she blacked out. "Y...yeah," she mumbled.

"I *really* wasn't trying to scare you. I know how touchy you upper street folks are about being down here."

She didn't trust him. People didn't come down this far. It wasn't *normal*. She herself landed here by accident, but it didn't look like the same thing brought this man down here. So he was down here for a *reason*, and what that reason might be, scared her.

She tried to stand.

He gently took her arm and helped her. Back on her feet, she looked around, holding herself.

"Name's Bryant," he said. "What's yours?"

"Look, I didn't mean to come down here. I just want to get back up top as soon as possible. Do you know where the keypad is?"

"Wow. That's a long name. Can I just call you 'Jessica' for short?"

She gasped. "How did you know my name?"

He pointed at her chest. "Your Intellecta access card."

She looked down at the white plastic card hanging around her neck. "Oh." The continued silence from her earcuff elevated her anxiety. She'd be *hours* catching up on her friends' updates. *If* she made it out of here alive.

"Jessica," he said, clearly trying her name out on his tongue, "I know where the keypad is. But you'll have to follow me, a stranger, though, through the dark." He grinned. "Can you do that?"

The only thing she knew she *couldn't* do was stay on this platform with a silent earcuff, no food, no water, and no hope of anyone finding her. "Well, I don't exactly have a choice, now, do I?" she snapped, scared to death to place her trust in a stranger who could off her where no one would ever think to look for her body.

His grin dropped, and a chord of compassion for his sincerity finally shot through her wall and stung her.

"I'm sorry," she amended. "I'm just scared." She shivered. Sunlight hadn't touched down this far in several hundred years.

"How did you get down here?" he asked with a sympathy she appreciated. It made him slightly more trustworthy.

"I didn't properly pronounce the number of the level I wanted. But I managed to stop it at forty-six."

"Not sooner?"

"I wasn't paying attention. But why are *you* down here?"

He shrugged lazily with one shoulder. "Science." He pointed up. "The keypad is about fifteen feet above our heads on the old platform. They moved the platform but not the keypad."

Jessica didn't like his one-word answer and his apparent refusal to clarify it. But then, he could have told her a complete detailed checklist of all he does and it still could have been lies.

"How do we get up there?"

"We'll have to take the stairs," he said. "It's a very roundabout way, but the only way."

Worry drew her eyebrows together.

He held out his arm. "Your eyes will have a hard time adjusting to the dark, I imagine, so hold on to me for now."

"We're going out in *that*?"

"Or you could stay here, I suppose."

She shook her head and latched onto his arm. He stepped out of the light. She held her breath, seeing absolutely nothing but naked, soul-eating darkness, fearing it was as thick as water and just as unbreathable.

She'd never been in darkness before, the productive city never sleeping and the lights never shutting off. Houses were made of a super lightweight, opaque material which did nothing to block the glow from the city lights all day and night. Everyone only still used the word "night" because it made it easy to determine which shift you worked.

She followed Bryant through the dark, walking on some metal platform she swore swayed side-to-side, having no idea how he could see, terrified he would take her back to his cannibal friends. She called out to her earcuff, and Bryant laughed.

"Signal stops at level 200," he said.

She couldn't stand her silent earcuff anymore. She *had* to have noise.

"How did you find me?" she asked, as if accusing him of a crime.

"Your RTP made such a racket, I walked three blocks over to discover what the hell was going on."

"Blocks?"

"It's...a measure of distance when you're on the ground."

"So what kind of 'science' do you do down here?" she tried again, because no one dropped below level 200 by choice, and this close to the ground? As long as you held a job in some capacity—or contributed to society with some artistic form—the government provided your living: food, water, and housing. There were no jails. Felons were executed once proven guilty and the bodies burned. Misdemeanors did community service. If they failed to do that, then they became a felon. The only reason anyone ended up living in Understreet was job loss and—point blank—their refusal to get another one. But that was Understreet. This was the *ground*. And level forty-six was basically the ground.

"Ah, Jessica, why the personal questions? You're going to get back to Upstreet and forget all about coming down here, so what's the point?"

"Silence scares me. My earcuff is *always* going off, so not to hear sound makes me horribly anxious, especially in the dark where I can't see anything."

"Okay. You tell me what you do for Intellecta, and if I like your answer, I'll tell you why I'm down here."

Anything for noise. "I'm a copywriter. Every month I come up with a new tagline to help people trust Intellecta's Intella-heart."

"Is it working? I did hear they were having a hard time selling the heart. Hell, I heard they can't *give* it away."

"Not since Ayden took it and ran. People believe the heart made him crazy, because who in their right mind would be miraculously healed from cancer, only to appear to hate it and run away? They think that it *must* be that the heart made him crazy. I'm sure you heard about Ayden?"

"Yes."

"Anyway, that's what I do for the company. Now, tell me about you." Her eyes started to adjust, making out walls, ramps, and…yes, lights. Tiny lights. Unused to anything but the loud glare of Upstreet lights, anything dimmer swallowed in darkness she did not immediately see. The constant light upside sent everyone eventually upgrading to robotic eyes. Jessica wondered if she wasn't getting to that point.

Bryant led her up a flight of rickety stairs clinging to the mortar of some stone building. She reached out and touched the ancient stone, something dug out of the earth, created by the earth.

Stone made a great foundation for raising a city, but became unstable at level fifty and above. A scientific creation called *salio*—strong and lightweight—created everything above that. Needed durability, however, used metal, including the magnetized rail system for the RTP.

They turned right at the top of the stairs. Able to see on her own now, she let go of him, dragging her hand along the rail.

When it became clear he wasn't going to answer her implied question, she said, "And you?"

"And me what?"

"What kind of scientific things bring you down to this level? You don't look old enough to have earned a commission from the city." He didn't respond for a long time, long enough that Jessica stopped caring about it. Finally, they reached the keypad illuminated by a tiny green light. Jessica hissed loudly in relief. Bryant was true to his word. Now she felt bad for being snappy with him earlier. She pressed her ring against the pad. It dinged once.

"It works," she breathed. Her ride was on the way. She'd be back up top in no time. Already she planned how to word her social update about this nightmare. She expected *hundreds* of comments. Maybe even enough to land on tomorrow's news.

"Oh," she said, "problem. The RTP is going to stop there." She pointed to the new platform beneath them.

"Then let's go. Quickly."

He took off at a brisk pace, Jessica keeping up now that she knew where they were going.

Back on the old platform, she looked up as the giant, white, pearl-looking Railed Transport Pod sunk down the rail toward them. It stopped and the door opened like a robotic arm welcoming her home.

"Thank you, Bryant." She'd mistrusted him earlier, but meant her gratitude now. "I would've literally died if you hadn't found me."

He laughed. "I can promise you wouldn't have died."

She disagreed, sliding into the RTP, feeling home already.

"I'm working on exactly one scientific theory," Bryant said, and it took Jessica a long moment before realizing he was answering her question from forever ago.

"Yeah? And what theory is that?"

"The existence of stars."

She watched him, unblinking, for a dreadfully long moment. "What are stars?"

He turned away from her, walking out of the light and back into the dark from which he had come.

She hit the button to close the door.

"Where is it you want to go?" asked the blessed voice of the RTP. "Level *twelve* thirty," she stressed with more clarity than she had given any word in her life.

"Acknowledged."

Jessica rested against the seat with a massive sigh of relief. As they rose higher, her earcuff tinkled, signifying a wireless connection. Sorely tempted to start recording her adventures of the night, she peeled away a layer of selfishness big enough to spend just a moment browsing the news to see if any traction had been made toward interest in the Intella-heart, which would be the direct result of Jephron's marketing. "Earcuff, play all of today's news starting at six p.m."

Anxious, she listened, filtering through a military update on the recently acquired Mexico State and rickety relations with the newly made Americans there, an electrical storm which wiped out half of Elko, Nevada's power grid, and...the Intella-heart.

"Intellecta's marketing team," the reporter said, "must have weaved a spell into their words because *ten thousand* people immediately called Intellecta to put their name on the next available date for surgery to install the lauded Intella-heart."

Jessica screamed, fists and feet punching and kicking the air. The news anchor continued, but Jessica stopped hearing, sending a message instead to Jephron, complimenting his *amazing* talent.

Ten thousand? Surely that wasn't even a full percent of the present population in Salt Lake, but when those people installed the heart and their family and friends witnessed the benefit for themselves...

Wow. Blown, she sat back with a hand to her hot forehead. *Wow.* And she had a small part to claim in that success. The bonus. The lives to be saved. She decided she *did* have an opinion about population control. She wanted everyone's lives to be *their* choice, just like her unused tagline had said.

Her tagline...she looked out the window as the city came alive around her with lights, *so* many vibrant, pulsing lights. What a perfect place to put her tagline, telling people their lives were their choice right after their decision to accept the Intella-heart. Like a reaffirmation they were making the right choice, defying the overpopulation naysayers by extending their lives without permission or shame. With a touch of rebellion, like the rain which made her think of the tagline in the first place.

It tore into her in a personal way when Haverick decided on the tagline that was not based on anything in particular. It shouldn't matter. She had still thought of it, still received pay for it. But she wanted *life is your choice* to go out in the advertisements, to blare across everyone's earcuff so every time she heard it she could be reminded of rain, a pure substance not designed, created, or even granted permission to exist by man. It just *was*. It had no master.

She opened herself to the network again to record, and she told her followers her tagline and how it reminded her of rain. "I work for Intellecta," she finished, "and life is your choice."

That taken care of, she dove right into her adventure of the night. She decided not to mention Bryant because no one would believe that she ran into another human down that far. She wouldn't have believed it either, except she knew she did not have the mental capacity to figure out how to guide herself through the dark on an unknown path to end up miraculously where she wanted to go.

She finished her recording and sat back to rest and listen to the updates she had missed that day, catching a message from Althea, her sister working for Loginetics in Las Vegas as one of their scientists. Althea helped build their competitive product, the BloodWise. It didn't replace the human heart, but was inserted inside it, which could be removed at any time.

"Congrats on the success of the Intella-heart," her sister's message said. "Even if I disagree that the heart should be replaced by a machine. There's still a copywriter spot open here...if you want it."

Jessica smiled and shook her head. She had been tempted in the past to move to Las Vegas and work close to her sister when Intellecta had fallen into stagnation after Ayden left. But tonight erased any temptation. Endless possibilities spread wide open for Intellecta's future. *Endless.* And she wanted a piece of that money-making pie.

Chapter Three

Her near-death questing through Understreet last night exhausted her badly enough that she finally acknowledged her alarm at 8:07…seven minutes late for work.

She shrieked and jumped out of bed. She ditched her morning ritual of listening to her earcuff and threw clothes on her body. Skipping breakfast, she barely acknowledged spilling her purse on her way out the door. She punched her ring into the keypad, dancing on her toes until the RTP arrived two minutes later.

"Where is it—"

"Intellecta! Intellecta!" she screamed over the unstoppable voice of the computer.

"Acknowledged."

The RTP sped off on its magnetic rail.

Jessica dug in her purse for a hair tie, but couldn't find one. It must've been one of the few things she accidentally dumped as she swept her purse off the counter. With nothing else she could further procrastinate with, she buzzed her earcuff to life, dreading the message from Haverick scolding her for being late.

Her earcuff notified her she had…*fifteen* missed calls?

What the literal hell?

They couldn't only be from Haverick. He would certainly call one time to inquire where she was, but…

"Play messages." She bunched her skirt inside a fist, bracing. "First message, twenty-three September, time 5:02 a.m., from Romona: 'Jessica? What the hell! Take your post *off* the social *right now* before anyone else sees. You hear me? Why the fuck won't you answer your phone?'"

What? Tears spread across her vision. *Which post? The one about my trip to Understreet or the one about the rain? There was nothing wrong with either of them.*

"Second message, twenty-three September, time 5:05 a.m.,

from Cory: 'Jessica, are you on drugs? Did you take any weird medications? I don't think Intellecta heard your post yet, so take it down now before you lose your job. If you need to vent, vent to me, not on social.' "

It is *about the rain!* Jessica's heart broke, one half going to her tagline being mocked, the other half to the massive upset she caused with it.

"Third message, twenty-three September, 5:26 a.m., from Haverick: 'Jessica, come to my office when you get to work.' "

No. No. No.

She ran out of time to listen to the other messages. They probably all said the same thing. The RTP stopped on Intellecta's platform.

Devastation watered her bones. Weakly, she left the RTP on shaking legs, not understanding why her tagline caused such an uproar. *I'll make the news alright. In infamy.*

She fought to keep her head up as she knocked on Haverick's door. "Come in!" he barked.

Tears burned her eyes as she twisted the handle and stepped inside. The fact that she didn't have time this morning to properly do her hair and makeup made this situation so much worse, because now she looked the very picture of ugly cry. Her dress even had wrinkles.

Haverick did not acknowledge her. Not even to offer her a seat. She stood petrified by his door while he finished listening to whatever he had programmed his earcuff to tell him.

He finally looked up, his face a mask of purple rage. "I should bring you up on charges!"

The tears broke. She always cried when people were mad at her. She grasped for an apology, but didn't know what to apologize for. She wanted to know *why* her social post upset everyone.

"I don't understand what I did wrong," she wailed. "I didn't think what I said was hurtful."

"Hurtful? *Hurtful?*" Haverick leapt from his chair and stomped across the room. She feared he'd swing his clenched fists. Worse, he towered over her and screamed. "I'm paying my damage control team overtime to stop your filth before it's shared or liked any more times. Why, *why* would you sabotage me?"

"I didn't do it to hurt the company!" she shouted back, horrified that she might lose her job no matter what she said or did in her defense. "I was just expressing my love for my tagline because it reminded me of the rain I saw the day I wrote it."

"What are you talking about?"

Jessica paused. Sniffed and wiped her eyes. "What are *you* talking about?"

"The other post you did last night."

"About my accidental trip to Understreet?"

"No. The *other* one."

She stared stupidly at him.

"You seriously don't remember? Were you high or something?"

Mutely, she shook her head. "Those are the only posts I made last night."

"Oh. *Denial,* is it? Now that you've been caught, you're going to deny it. Recorder, play Jessica Halwater's post made at 4:59 a.m. this morning.

A second later, Jessica's voice came on the speakers.

"As you all know, I work for Intellecta. I'm the copywriter. Currently, they have me writing content to pitch their controversial Intella-heart. You all need to know the truth. The heart doesn't work. That's to say, it *will* pump blood like the real thing, but it won't cure any diseases like Intellecta touts. It's a scam. But by the time you realize you've been rooked, Intellecta will already have your money and there is no return policy. Don't buy into this scam. That's why Ayden ran away. He didn't want Intellecta *silencing* him to keep him from telling the truth."

The message clicked off.

Hot mortification swept over her. "I didn't say that!"

"You're fired."

Jessica's lungs lost all air. Her vision sparkled. Her knees gave out and she sat down hard on the floor, swooning until the threatening unconsciousness cleared. Two security officers entered the room. "I demand an appeal!"

Security grabbed her arms.

They escorted her out of Haverick's office. Her personal effects had been gathered into a box out of her office by a nervous-looking clerk waiting just outside Haverick's door.

Jessica didn't fight them, but she had no strength to carry herself, so they half dragged her down the linoleum hallway to the platform outside. All the while, she racked her brains. *Sabotage Haverick? Someone sabotaged* me!

Security keyed for an RTP, and a blue, triple-seater arrived. They helped her inside—helped themselves inside—and the RTP took off. She sobbed. She was going to lose her house. Her *earcuff*. Government said if you did not benefit society in either art or production, they weren't going to let you benefit with a house...and they were going to disconnect her earcuff.

Her sobs turned into banshee wails.

"Shut up," the security officer barked.

She shut her lips, covering them with her mouth, and sobbed into her knees.

The RTP stopped in front of her house.

The door opened, and with a pressured prompting from one of the security guards, she stepped out. They got out as well, one of them carrying the box they'd used to clean up her office. The RTP, owned by Intellecta, remained, waiting for them to return to it.

"Hand over your badge," one said.

Jessica did so, returning her arms to hug herself as if the hot day chilled her.

In what sounded like well-recited dialogue, he said, "You have been officially fired from Intellecta. You are not allowed inside the premises. You are not allowed to claim any benefits from Intellecta, which means you forfeit your house and access to the WebNet, so you will be disconnected from the ring and earcuff. All will still be available to you for the next seven days, giving you time to contest Intellecta's findings with Jobtech Services concerning your termination. If you are still found to be at fault by the end of seven days and are unable to obtain another job before then, you will be evicted and disconnected." Like robots themselves, the two security officers sat back in the RTP and it whirled away.

Jessica couldn't think with the thunder in her head, limbs stiff with dread. *Jobtech...I need to speak with Jobtech...*Filled with rage she had never known, she punched her ring so hard into the keypad, all four fingers screamed in pain.

The RTP arrived. Leaving her box of office effects on the platform in front of her house, she commanded the vehicle to take her to the Center of Wrongs Undone, which she translated into "Jobtech" for the RTP's computer.

The vehicle stopped in front of the building. She dismounted, storming across the platform to the building's doorless entry. The massive chamber held dozens of desks in military-like formations. Two bodies occupied every one—the Jobtechnician and the complainant—so Jessica pulled her number and sat on a bench holding twenty other people. It looked very possible she wasn't going to be seen for three days, but people often got impatient and left early, voiding their spot in line. Some were lucky enough to leave and come back the next day and still keep their spot in line, but Jessica didn't feel tired, hungry, or thirsty. Perfectly content to sit it out right there for the next week.

Someone slid onto the bench next to her.

"Intellecta fired you?" a familiar voice asked.

She looked up to find Bryant's calm eyes assessing her. He had appeared ghost-like in the dark, like some haunt over the city's buried history. In the daylight, up where normal people lived, she saw color in his cheeks, and his eyes were nothing more special than a boring, mortal blue.

She wanted to ask how he ended up in the same Jobtech as her at the same time she arrived, what job he had been fired from, but selfish heat swallowed her and she latched onto his question like a virus in a computer and poured her frustration onto him.

"I *swear* I didn't record that post. I know it was my voice, but I was perfectly sober last night and was so tired I went to bed. I don't even *feel* that way about Intellecta, so how could I think that lie up?"

"You know that's going to be hard to prove to the Jobtechnicians," he said like some sage come to torment her more with hopelessness.

"I was hacked. Someone hacked my WebNet and used a voice modifier to make it sound like me."

"And why would someone do that?"

"I don't know! Maybe they want my job."

"Do you get paid enough to be the envy of even a more common job?"

Intellecta was sure to make—emphasis on *was*—money off that last marketing tactic. A lot of money. Her current day-to-day salary paid her comfortably, but not obscenely. There's no telling if anyone would sign up for the Intella-heart after the post that got her fired, so anyone who replaced her position would still not likely share a chunk of Intellecta's would-have-been victory, especially since they were not the ones who copywrote for the campaign.

"No."

"So that's out."

"Look, why are you here anyway, Bryant? I didn't see you pull a number so you're not in line for anything."

"I think I know how to help you."

For the first time in an hour, her heart started beating again and new life flooded too brightly for his non-committal offer of hope. "How?"

"I told you I was doing scientific research in Understreet. I'm not the only one working down there. I happened to have overheard some population control villains talking about sabotaging you, since they overheard you saying you worked for

Intellecta. I came up here to tell you so you could have proof to give to the Jobtechs. You know they will hear every case, but won't investigate it unless you give them some lead."

"I'd have to take a police force to Understreet with me to get my hackers to talk, and the police won't come with me either unless I have proof!"

"I'll escort you down to Understreet and gather the proof with you. We could have it by tonight and, seeing your number, you probably won't even lose your place in line."

"Oh, would you? That would be so great!"

He nodded and stood, offering her a hand. Outside, he used his ring to summon an RTP, and Jessica spent the few moments waiting for it basking in relief. She would get her job back. Something niggled in her brain to not trust a stranger she found in Understreet so easily, but he *was* connected to the WebNet since he summoned an RTP with his ring, which meant he had a job to give him access to the WebNet, which meant he *was* the scientist he claimed to be.

Their RTP arrived.

"Where is it you would like to go?" asked the computer as both of them sat inside.

"Ground zero," Bryant said.

Chapter Four

Jessica squealed. "*What?*"

The RTP shot forward.

"*Ground freaking zero?*"

"Yes."

"I don't want to go down there!"

"Don't you want your proof?"

She slumped back in her seat, suspicious that she'd been kidnapped. The RTP dipped downward, the inside rotating so their heads always remained up.

The second she saw something hanky, she would summon

an RTP to bring her back up top. That is, only if *ground freaking zero* was not anything like her last ruinous trip and there was not an easily identifiable keypad for her to summon one. It would take absolute days under physical strain climbing back up all those stairs.

She wanted to put out a post on social about her whereabouts to her friends so they would know where to look for her, but she didn't want Bryant overhearing the recording. She thought all this as the RTP lowered deeper and deeper into the city. If She couldn't see out the black windows. The RTP slowed and stopped. The door opened.

She didn't move.

"You going to get out?"

She had no reason to discount Bryant's helpfulness—despite him insisting they hit the bottom of the world. And he *did* help her out last night. But neither could she discount the stories, myths, legends, and rumors of what prowled on the dirt she was about to stand on.

She might die today. Better get it over with.

She stepped out. Bryant followed. The door closed, and her last chance at immediate escape rose up through the dark.

Dark. Everywhere. Her eyes would still take a moment adjusting before those tiny lights she saw last night would become visible to her. Those tiny lights from whatever wires and electronics still thrived down here, pumping blood to the heart above. If Bryant had taken her into the sealed case of a computer, it would feel the same. Except the smell. And the silence.

She had been starkly introduced to the silence last night, but she blamed that awful void on her wirelessly disconnected earcuff. Disconnected once again, she noticed something her panic of last night failed to notice.

Upstreet *blared.*

The constant chatter of her earcuff, the hum of RTPs sliding over rails, the constant pulse of electricity powering everything from lights—so many lights—to the 3D printed food machines.

Down here? Nothing but Bryant's shoes scuffing the dirt as he dug around in his bag.

And the dirt...smelled. A real smell. Not man-made. Salt Lake had eliminated pollution hundreds of years ago by creating transportation geared for rails and magnets and factories opting for methods that never produced smoke or gas. So Upstreet didn't have a smell, unless you stepped into a bakery, or a business that utilized air fresheners.

But down here, she described the smell as wet darkness, something which had been here before man and would remain even after man ceased to exist. It smelled natural. And, she supposed, it smelled like dirt was supposed to smell like, even though she couldn't have an opinion on if it should smell like something else.

Bryant clicked on a flashlight. She realized she didn't bring anything for herself, save a purse holding makeup, an emergency tampon, and maybe a pen, but she thought she'd dumped it out with her hair tie. She didn't even have smart shoes. Or the WebNet. She'd fallen into Bryant's complete mercy. Keeping a grip on his arm, he led her through the dark. Soon, her eyes made out gray shapes beyond the flashlight's beam, giving edges to old buildings used for structural bones to the city above it.

They must have walked the length of two skyscrapers before Bryant turned her toward a stone fortress that glimmered when his flashlight streaked across it. Yawning square holes in the walls might be windows, and might have once been sealed with glass—if she recalled her history class in high school accurately. They walked up three steps into a chamber filled with light.

Inside, wires chased all across the walls and ceiling like a complex, multi-railed RTP system, the beads of light along the wires could have been miniature RTPs themselves, all connecting to twenty or so computer monitors fixed randomly on tables in no thoughtful pattern.

Three people stood when they entered. Jessica took a voluntary step back. Bryant motioned the three to approach: a girl with pink hair, a lanky, baby-faced guy with pale skin, and an extremely overweight man reeking of sweat.

"Everyone," Bryant announced, "this is Jessica."

"Hello," they all said in varying degrees of tones and sincerity. "Hi," she said nervously back.

Bryant pointed to the pink-haired girl. "This is Hacker. She broke into your WebNet social feed."

"Ah, what?"

"And this is Copycat," he said about the lanky kid who grinned lazily. "He can mimic any voice, boy or girl. Show her."

Copycat opened his mouth, and in perfect imitation of Jessica's voice, said, "Life is your choice."

Jessica's jaw dropped.

"He's the one who mimicked your voice on your social post. And the fat one is—"

Jessica slammed both arms against Bryant's chest with the force of paper blowing in the wind. "*You* sabotaged me?"

"Yes."

"You...you..." She couldn't quite call him a liar because he did fulfill his promise to take her to the hackers. She pulled back and just screamed, dropping to her knees in a pathetic mess on the cold stone floor. "You *ruined* me!"

"You're not ruined. You have your right to appeal and they'll launch an investigation and find the voice is not actually yours."

"*Why* did you sabotage me?"

"We need you to see something, and we need you to tell the rest of America."

"See what?"

"The stars."

"But I have no idea what they are!"

"Stars are lights in the sky."

"Right, because *those* are different than the lights I see every day."

"You also get water in the city, but it still does not compare to rain."

He winked.

Winked, as if sabotaging her was all a joke and she stood at the butt of it.

She jumped to her feet. "You are a monster and I will do *nothing* to help you. Thank you for giving me the evidence I need to get my life back." She spun on her heel and walked outside into the grainy gray darkness.

They had made a couple turns from the point of debarkation from the RTP. She could make it back.

Bryant caught up to her, walking backward so he could face her. "Yes, I am a monster for deceiving you. But if I hadn't made it so you were completely beholden to me, you wouldn't have agreed to work with me."

"I'm *not* working for you and I am *not* beholden to you."

"No? You think you can make it back to the keypad to call for an RTP?"

"Watch me."

"I'll just find another Intellecta representative. But then, you'll never hear my *shocking* secret." Both eyebrows lifted in a wicked grin.

"You're bluffing."

"I know what happened to Ayden."

She stuttered, then said it anyway. "Still bluffing."

"He's alive."

"...Still bluffing."

"Suit yourself." He spun around, walking off with the only flashlight.

She stopped, staring into the darkness ahead and the retreating light behind.

"What's so special about your stars that all of America needs to know about them?" she asked.

He spun around to face her, walking backward. "The stars aren't the point. What the point is, is you have to shut the lights off to see them."

"What lights?"

"The city lights. All of them. They cause too much glow on the atmosphere and block out the stars."

"Shut off all the lights? You'd have to cut off the power!" "Yes."

"You *can't* do that."

His grin infuriated her even as it shrunk the farther away he walked backward. "Why not?"

"Because...RTPs will stop moving. The *network* will silence. Life support machines will stop." He'd walked so far she had to shout.

"Life support machines have backup power. They will be alright."

"I won't help you shut off the lights!" She stomped her foot.

It must have been her foot stomp that did it, because he paused, and slowly turned. "How much do you know about the Intella-heart?"

"That it saves lives."

"I mean...you're just a copywriter, right? Not one of their scientists? Not one of those who know the *real* secrets to the Intella-heart's power?"

"If I were one of their godly scientists, they would have been mandated to provide me a severance package when they fired me. If it's a scientist you want, take me back up and I'll give my recommendation to the scientist you should kidnap next."

"You can down hear willingly. I didn't kidnap you."

"I won't help you shut off the lights!"

"I didn't ask you to help us shut off the lights, now, did I? That's what my team is for. We've been hacking the system for three years and everything is good to go. We were just waiting for a representative from Intellecta. And then you mistakenly dropped down here yesterday. One might say they don't believe in coincidences."

"I won't help you!"

"Hope you make it back to the RTP. I won't be able to find you if you get lost." He spun around, taking the only light.

It didn't take her long to decide her eyes hadn't adjusted well enough, that she *didn't* know how to make it back to the RTP, and terror over getting lost powered her feet to pound after Bryant.

He must have heard her tromping footsteps because he stopped, waiting for her.

"I'm not promising to help you," she gasped, regaining her breath. "You will after you see what I have to show you tomorrow night." "Your stupid stars aren't going to change my mind."

"Your stupid rain changed your mind about your tagline." She opened her mouth, but no sound came out. *The villain!* He'd snared her good and true, first when he smoothly convinced her to follow him down here, and now by using her own words against her. A single word pierced her irritation. *Ayden.* And for that, she would seek justice against Bryant.

They walked back into the building with all the lights and wires. Bryant's three team members glanced over their shoulders at her re-arrival and went back to ignoring her again.

Bryant pointed to the fat teammate who handled so many exposed wires Jessica feared he would set himself on fire. "And that is Sizzle," Bryant said. "Our electricity specialist."

"So what's your made-up name, *Bryant*?" she sneered.

"Bryant *is* my made-up name." He spread his arms wide. "We live here, so find a spot of floor and it's yours."

"What is this place?" Behind the clumps of sprawling wires, Jessica noticed the wall was not the same stone she had seen outside. The wall behind the wires held narrow blocks of something, all in varying heights and colors lined along shelves.

"This is Salt Lake City's County Library," he said.

"Library? As in...those are *books*?"

"Yes."

"Oh goodness." History did well sifting through every single detail of the past, clinging to those few moments which had the greatest impact on humanity where cultures changed and society either conquered or failed. Books were noted 900 years ago as one such failure.

"Feel free to read whatever you find. I actually find them quite enjoyable."

"You've *read* them?"

"Why not? I'm an outcast from society as is, so I don't feel inclined to follow rules. I really don't understand what the upset is about books anyway. I didn't find anything offensive about them."

"How can you *not* have found them offensive? They were *banned*, Bryant. Every single one of those horrible authors inserted some biased opinion about their feelings on gender or race, and they had the *gall* to mask it over as 'an enjoyable read.' Barbaric!"

Bryant sighed. "But you see, I've read them. They're just made-up stories. You create stories on your social posts, do you not?"

"But I'm not insensitive to gender or race."

"I'm not insensitive either. I got bored out of my mind living down here and desperately needed something to do. I quite like reading, actually. Read something while you're here."

"I can't read."

He looked up at the ceiling. "Oh."

"I'm actually surprised *you* know how to read."

"Some people read, Jessica. Some jobs need it."

"Only *poor* jobs."

He folded his arms and looked around the chamber. "Was I this rude when I lived topside?" he asked his team.

"You certainly would have been had someone *ruined* your life," Jessica said.

"Are you hungry? I think you're hungry. Have a seat somewhere and I'll bring you something to eat." Bryant whirled around and walked through an adjoining doorway.

Jessica found a space against the wall of the main chamber that wasn't as tangled with wires as the rest of it. She sat down and hugged her knees. Bryant reemerged a moment later with a thin sleeping pad, blanket, and a wrapped package. He handed all of it to her—the package turned out to be food—and left without a word exchanged between them.

The labeling on the food declared he'd gotten it from a vendor who purchased it from the synthetic protein manufacturers. A step down from her usual 3D printed food manufactured local in Salt Lake. This package manifested its point of origin as New York. So probably lacking preservatives. Yuck.

She longed for her earcuff, hearing only madness in the silence she still was not used to. If it wasn't for the steady beeps and drones of the monitors, she would have literally lost her mind. She'd have to take a full day just to catch up on her friends' status.

Unable to know what time it was, she laid on the thin foam pad, tired. But the busy atmosphere around her, the uncomfortable pad, and her rage at Bryant for literally ruining her life kept her solidly awake.

She watched all four of them. Hacker blew bubbles with her gum while all ten fingers roamed deftly across the keyboard. Jessica wondered what caused them to fall from society and end up in Understreet. Crime? Loss of a job? Both of those were so rare she'd never heard of that happening to anyone, since the government knew that displaced people caused more problems.

Nine hundred years ago when everyone still lived on the ground, the city mayor decided to round up all the homeless people and dump them on a street called the Rio Grande. With all the poverty and desperateness crammed together, crime shot through the roof and they then had to go in and break them all up. It was bad enough schools still discussed it in history class. Since learning from that mistake, the government paid work recruiters to search all levels of the city for jobless people. So unemployment was rare. Jessica didn't doubt she'd either get her job back or another one, but likely not before she was...she choked...*disconnected.* Intellecta would only continue paying for her network for a week.

She watched the team of four work at the monitors. She briefly considered sabotaging them to prevent their act of terror, but Bryant said he knew where Ayden was. If he told her where to find him...she sat up straighter, heart pounding. Haverick would hire her back! *And* she'd get the cops down here before they could cut the power.

Relief flooded her in a warm flush. Oh, yes. She'd go along with Bryant's plan. By tomorrow night, she'd have her job back.

Chapter Five

"Jessica."

She shifted under the blanket. "What?"

"It's morning. Do you want breakfast?"

She sat up, motivated with the approaching moment when Bryant told her where Ayden was. He handed her another wrapped package of food. "Why do you need someone from Intellecta?" she asked, tearing open the package.

"To expose them."

"Expose them over what?"

"Over what I'm going to show you tonight when I shut off the lights."

"I'm not helping. *Terrorist.*"

"Even if I showed you where Ayden is right now?"

"Show me him first and then I'll decide." Lie. She'd already decided she wouldn't be part of them shutting off the city lights. She'd gather her proof of Ayden and vanish before Bryant convinced her again she was beholden to him.

"I'll do that. Let's go."

Taking her food with her, she followed him outside into a wall of darkness, trailing behind his flashlight beam as he navigated the landscape. Not far down he entered another building, the flashlight beam sliding across a canvas draped over a bulky item. He pulled the canvas off, revealing a clunky, metal contraption. She couldn't guess what it was used for.

Bryant swung a long leg over the center of the machine as if he meant to ride it as a horse like what she'd seen in art exhibits. He fingered around the machine, and an enormous roar busted her eardrums the same time a blinding light on the front of it turned on.

She shrieked and backed up, covering both ears. "What is that?"

"A motorcycle." He had to raise his voice. "I found a book on it in the library and fixed it up."

"Is that a..." *Impossible.* "A *gas* engine?"

"Yes."

Old gas motors caused emissions that destroyed air quality, and the gas to fuel it nearly ran out. The motorcycle rolled forward up to her on two black circles. He tossed a chin over his shoulder. "Get on."

Excitement sparked inside her at the danger of something controlled by a man and not a computer.

She slid onto the seat behind him.

"Pick up your feet."

She did so, both hands wrapped around him as he gunned the engine and it moved forward with the same force she felt in an RTP. The single headlight cut a yellow path down a flat black surface, chunks of ancient asphalt heaved and cracked. They came to an intersection, passing beneath poles Jessica believed once hung stoplights used to guide vehicles when to stop and go and turn, each vehicle controlled by a human. How all those people navigated these ancient streets at the same time made Jessica shake her head in disbelief. The impossible patterns of passing each other, crossing these intersections. The deaths caused when someone turned too soon, or too late.

Bryant drove confidently, making rights and lefts on the black surface, Jessica watching with an intensity that nearly made her forget what brought her down to the ground in the first place.

Finally, he slowed to a stop next to an RTP rail diving straight into the dirt and got off the motorcycle.

"We're taking an RTP?" she asked, dismounting alongside him.

"Yes."

"Why not use the one we took yesterday?"

"This rail is closer to where I want to end up. Less time for me being on Upstreet."

"And that's a problem because..."

He didn't answer, instead walking to the wall near the rail and punching a ring into the glowing pad. She doubted his ring connected to the network. Likely another hack by him and his team.

"When you first deceived me to come down here," Jessica sneered, "you called yourselves *population control villains.* You want population control?"

"I agree population should be regulated, but the methods others want to implement are mass-execution style."

Jessica recalled a similar conversation in the bathroom at Intellecta.

"So we are called villains to those who want mass executions where we are against it."

The RTP arrived, stopping mere inches off the dirt and opening its door. Jessica slid into its comforting familiarity.

"Where is it you want to go?" the computer asked.

"1165."

Jessica held her breath as the RTP rose, waiting for the little ding in her earcuff to signal her connection to the network...*ding!* Her next breath commanded her earcuff to play all the social posts she had missed. Already her life felt nearly back to normal as she commented on each post as if Bryant weren't sharing the same space with her.

The RTP stopped and Bryant got out. She sighed and stopped playing her earcuff. She stepped onto a platform that branched into walkways connecting several living quarters stacked top and bottom, all the same size and color, designated differently only by large numbers stamped next to the door. Bryant walked along a ramp, stopping in front of house number 811.

"Ayden lives here?" she asked to make sure. In case Bryant decided to ditch her for whatever reason, she could still bring Intellecta here.

"Yes." He faced her. "I'm going to go inside, but I want you to stay right here."

"How do I know you're not making it up?"

"If you *watch*," he said, lowering his gaze to match his intensity, "it will become very clear to you."

"All right." If he *was* making this up, she wasn't too far below Intellecta's level. Ah! Her own bed tonight. Smiling, she watched as Bryant walked up the porch and knocked on the door.

The door opened. Jessica didn't see the woman's face beyond the doorway, but she saw her arms wrap around Bryant's neck, and heard her call out his name with a half-sob.

Only, she didn't call him Bryant.

Jessica leaned on the rail, knees threatening to give out.

The man who called himself Bryant walked into the house.

The woman who called him Ayden closed the door behind him.

Chapter Six

Bryant's footsteps clattered on the metal platform. He stopped next to her. She didn't lift her head.

"Seeing as you're still here and *didn't* immediately leave to tell Intellecta where they can find me, tells me there is something else you want more instead."

"Why did you run away?"

"There are things about this heart Intellecta will not tell anyone. It's taken me three years of research, guesses, and theories to conclude how the heart works, and it's not a nice thought."

"How then?"

"It's just a theory, one that will either be proved or disproved the moment we shut off the city lights tonight."

"So it's not because you want to see the stars. You just want to see if your theory is right."

"If it is right...that's where you come in. You tell America the truth. If I'm wrong, well, then I really do want to see the stars all the same."

"What's your theory?"

"Would you have believed I was Ayden if I had just told you?"

"...No."

"Which is why I had a third, unbiased, unknowing party admit it out loud to where you could hear."

"You could have set this up in advance."

He pulled down the collar of his shirt. The collar stretched over a stylized "I" burned over his heart. She stared too hard at it, some strange emotion filling her veins with acid. Intellecta's first heart pulsed beneath that "I". During this new shift in her reality, she bizarrely wondered if the "I" was further Intellecta marketing or to notify medical responders whether they worked with an organ or a machine.

"I did set you up." He released his shirt collar. "That was my mother. I've known my entire life she would always call me 'Ayden' every time I came unexpectedly for a visit. I brought you here to *see*, for the same reason you're coming with me to *see* if I am right. Otherwise, you'll be predisposed to bias. *Especially* since you love Intellecta so much."

She disagreed, but she didn't leave him either. Doubt seeped into the cracks in her heart, telling her Ayden would not have run away, choosing to live on the ground, if there wasn't something driving him to it.

Silence followed them back to the RTP, back to the ground, back to the banned library, and she neither turned on her earcuff, opened her mouth to speak, or breathed too heavily. She sat in devastating silence, trying to convince herself she still wanted her job back.

Chapter Seven

They rode out in silent ceremony, Ayden's three team members on their own motorcycles, in a line, as they traced the ancient streets until they caught one that turned them west, away from the city's thick foundation.

The pillars holding the city above their heads thinned more and more until nothing spread above them but the hazy sky reflecting city lights. It came in patches where they drove under more naked sky than city. Jessica couldn't fathom this team shutting off the lights.

She held onto Ayden's waist, a scarf wrapped around her mouth to keep from swallowing bugs—so he told her.

The roar of engines lulled her into a strange calm she almost enjoyed, somehow able to hear the hush of the Understreet night beyond the purr of the motorcycles.

After several miles and several turns—guided by the broken roads—they pulled up to the city's namesake lake. Ayden killed the engine and dismounted. She followed.

His team grabbed their bags and bustled toward the water. Giant pipes big enough for them to have driven through reached toward the center of the lake in all directions. A skyscraper towered in the middle where all the pipes met, lit with blue lights spiraling down around it, mirroring the lights along the massive pipes on the ground.

Ayden did not follow his team as they scuttled across one of the pipes, heading to the skyscraper. They passed under a tall pole, which was topped with a glassy sphere. Each pipe reaching toward the skyscraper had one.

"Ayden!" Jessica thrust her finger at the sphere. "It's a camera!"

He looked to where she pointed. "There's no help for it." He dropped to his knees with his bag, ripping open a zipper with aggressive force. "Which is why my team is *running* to the skyscraper."

"Who do you think is watching?"

"Likely the police and maintenance."

"So when the power is cut…"

"Yes."

Jessica watched Ayden pull a camera of his own out of his bag. Jessica had only seen cameras of that style in history books. Modern cameras were live-linked to the WebNet to store photos for later editing, or immediate posting. Though society consumed media primarily through audio, there was a niche for visual as well, observed from the televisions throughout the city by journalists, reporters, and social influencers gone viral.

The camera Ayden pulled out was the last model to not be live-linked. A photographer with a camera of that model would have to take it within proximity to a wireless router to connect it to the WebNet, because all data was stored inside the camera. The positive side was it could still record without power, whereas modern ones could not. Modern ones needed that live-link. Which is why those old models were replaced, because the city's power, of course, would *never* go out.

Jessica sat on the ground and hugged her knees, turning away from the camera even though she'd already shown her face to it nice and pretty.

Now her face would blow up every screen in Salt Lake on their Most Wanted list. She wasn't ready for this vigilante life.

She searched about in her angry brain to find words to blame Ayden for it. But she couldn't find the words, because every step up to this point, this very point where she now sat in the dirt, punching her fist into it, she took with a clear, sober mind.

Getting in the RTP with Ayden after the Jobtech center. Staying with them in the library last night. Swinging her leg over the motorcycle and hugging Ayden's middle as he gunned the machine to the lake. All of it she did with a choice. So the only person she could blame was herself.

Topping the tripod with the camera, Ayden stood in front

of it. "My name is Ayden Carfor. I am the first and only patient of Intellecta's to own their Intella-heart." He lifted his shirt to show the *I*, and dropped it. "Please watch, and you will find out exactly why the Intella-heart is fatal."

"Fatal?" Jessica asked, not caring that the camera—all the cameras—recorded her too.

He sat down in the salt-crusted dirt and rocks making up the lake's shore, still directly in front of the camera. He looked at her. "If my theory proves true...well, just watch."

"Is there *anything* you're willing to tell me?"

His eyes narrowed.

She spread her arms. "I'm certainly not going to *run* back to Intellecta with all your secrets. And forget about me knowing how to drive that motorcycle."

He looked back across the water. She spied in his posture that he didn't want to admit his theory out loud. Fear crept into his scrunched forehead.

"I ran away," he said at long last, "because I didn't feel human. I was part machine, part of something created by man."

"The heart saved your life."

Before she could rant about his ingratitude, he said, "No one asked me if that's what I wanted."

"No one asked *me* if I wanted someone to hack my network and get me *fired*!"

"So you understand how pissed I was too."

"But this is your *life*. You have no right to be pissed about someone saving your stupid life."

"Don't I? Imagine if it were you, Jessica. Your heart gutted out of your chest and replaced by a machine."

"I'd be grateful."

"Would you love the rain just as much if man created it?"

She bunched salty dirt in both fists, fighting a horrible urge to throw it at him because of his constant reminders about her stupid love for the rain.

"Your silence tells me you would not love it as much. That's how this Intella-heart makes me feel about my life."

"Then, are you saying that those with robotic eyes and prosthetic limbs hold no human value to you?"

He stared into the distance with his arms folded a long moment. A breeze picked up and ruffled their clothes, wafting salt at them from across the Salt Flats. "I contracted cancer. I don't know how. Might be because of the recycled water and the chemicals used to purify it. Maybe from the lab-grown meat and 3D printed food. No telling. My parents both worked at one of those 'poor' jobs..." He looked askance at her. She looked away. "And were threatened with financial ruin to pay for treatment. I refused to let them do that to themselves. I told them my wishes were to let me die comfortably at home. I would die comforted that they would still be financially secure. The last week of my life, the cancer put me into a coma.

"While I was under, my parents petitioned all their social channels asking if anyone could donate or help somehow with healing me. I had prohibited them from doing so sooner, so they took advantage of my unconsciousness. Intellecta responded to them, and offered them a free heart. Against my wishes and without my permission, they donated my body to Intellecta, and they cut me open. I woke and was informed that payment for my heart would be nothing more difficult than being interviewed about my miraculous recovery by all the news outlets and sharing my new, healthy, daily lifestyle on my socials.

"Jessica, I was livid. I have nothing against, and even support, those who choose prosthetics. *Choose.* Maybe you're okay having someone else dictate your life. I am not. If I chose to die, that was my choice."

Without warning, Jessica's favorite line—*life is your choice*—beamed through her head. Not in the way she intended, she still could not deny both meanings.

"What Intellecta did was reduce my life down to the value of a billboard since I had to 'pay back' the heart by marketing it for them. 'The Intella-heart worked! Get one for yourself!' 'The Intella-heart cured my cancer. Get your heart today, go back to work tomorrow'. And Jessica, I didn't want to be a billboard.

"I also didn't want to feel like I had to earn my life. God gave it to me freely without any obligation on me to pay for it. I didn't want the value of my life to be force-earned by a company invested in me only monetarily. I was so livid that I ran away to Understreet. I ran and ran until my earcuff disconnected from the WebNet. I kept running. My best friend, whom you know as Copycat, followed me. I tried running from him too, but he kept up. I didn't take an RTP. I took the stairs. In my energized rage—and, I suppose, with the energy of the new Intella-heart—I still don't know how many levels I ran down before I stopped running and walked. I kept walking down, thinking, in my rebellion, to kill myself to show my parents I would *still* fulfill my wishes and prevent Intellecta from using me as a tool. I walked so far down I didn't need to kill myself, because the Intella-heart stopped beating."

Jessica jolted. "Stopped? Just like that?"

"*Not* just like that. I had started feeling really weak, breathless, and bizarre before I collapsed on the stairs. Copycat didn't feel a pulse. He picked me up and hauled my body up to the closest flat spot on the stairs because he needed me flat and level to administer CPR. Even walking a few steps upward, my heart started beating again and I woke up. Copycat told me what had happened, but I insisted on continuing down. I reached the same point I collapsed, and collapsed again. He picked me up, carried me up the stairs, and the heart started again. That's the moment I started developing my theories on the Intella-heart."

"So…if being so far in Understreet stopped your heart, how is it you are still alive after living here?"

He pulled two pucks out of his pocket, used for wireless transfer of electricity and internet, as if in answer to her question. It was the smallest model available, only able to link to a single device at a time. One of them must be what was powering the camera on the tripod, since even his old model camera was powered by wireless electricity. Batteries became obsolete a hundred years ago. She assumed the second puck powered his earcuff, but she noticed he wasn't wearing it.

"Those pucks don't answer my question."

"It does."

"Will you stop with the suspense and just tell me?"

"I want to prove if my theory is true, first. Which, I one hundred percent think it is. You only have a few more moments to wait." He pinched his lips together. "I will say, Jessica, that, though my new Intella-heart put me in a rage, I imagine I still would have eventually accepted it and moved onward with a fulfilling life, if not, however, for the theory I developed that moment I collapsed on the stairs."

They sat in silence a long while, Jessica hugging her knees, assuming the team had failed to turn off the lights, failed to cut the power. A small part of her felt sad about it.

Then the blue lights dimmed, and a distant whirring noise she had not noticed until now, died down.

"We did it…" Ayden stood.

She stood too, looking at the city surrounding the lake, watching all the lights blink off.

She stepped backward toward Ayden, scared of the oppressive dark. "Jessica…look…"

Look at…She gasped, her chin lifting…lifting…her feet would leave the ground any second, pulled into an endless, eternal, unimaginable expanse where heaven and earth married, where man and his creations, pomp, and reputation stood no taller than the minuscule salt cubes beneath her shoes amongst it all.

This is where her rain had fallen from.

Stars. Millions upon millions of them in the sky.

Stars. Tiny lights brighter than glitter, crimson and blue mist smeared across it all in a swirl of color no computer could copy.

Stars. Dressing around the sliver of moon like a wedding gown.

Stars. Did man intentionally blare out the sky with so many lights, so they could ignore the behemoth above them and pretend this thing out of their control did not exist?

"Wha–" She didn't know how to ask, didn't know how to stop her betraying heart from telling her *this* was not made by man. And now she understood why Ayden didn't want the Intella-heart. She couldn't go back to the city, not when she knew what it kept masked from her. She wanted to live on the ground and learn how to read, ride motorcycles, show others the sky, to bring back again the art man had lost, the art of photographing and painting the natural world and wildlife before they died off, of trees before man uprooted them all, of the mountains before skyscrapers buried them, of the rivers before man choked them.

She wanted all the stars. Wanted to drink them. Crush them into her skin. She wanted photographs of the stars to hang in her house. She wanted to paint them and share them and look at the real ones every night, be swept away into their dreaming, wrap herself in their endless eternity.

It took her a moment of disconnected reality to realize Ayden had moved suddenly next to her, and she looked down to see he had collapsed to the shore.

"Ayden!" She scattered salt as she dropped next to him on her knees.

He sat up on one elbow, clutching his chest with his other hand, panting. "I was right."

"Right about what?"

"My Intella-heart. It's powered by the city's power grid."

Her own heart pounded five solid times before she realized what that meant.

"You're going to die!" She stood up and screamed across the water. "Turn the power back on! Ayden is dying! Turn it—"

"Jessica, stop. I prepared for this. It's why I visited my parents this morning."

"They're okay with you killing yourself?"

"They don't know. I've lied to them about what I've been doing the last three years I..." His breath hitched. "Threatened if they told anyone about me, I'd stop visiting and disappear forever."

She turned her panicked shouting on him. "Why would Intellecta do this? Can you imagine how many people would die if they all had that heart and the power…" Her shouting died, everything connecting. In a single breathless exhale, she said, "Population control."

He nodded, despite the pain wrenching his expression.

"Population," she said. She couldn't think of any other words. Couldn't breathe.

Ten thousand, the news anchor said. Intellecta would wait for more, hundreds of thousands more, before they revealed the secret in a failing blip of lights.

Ayden's face lost all color, the heart failing to regulate his blood flow. "The camera is recording all of this." His breathing labored. "Upload it as soon as the power…comes back…on…."

Reclined on his elbow, he laid on his back, eyes glazed with starlight as he looked up.

And stopped blinking.

Chapter Eight

Dead.

In front of her.

On the edge of a lake with no WebNet connection to call for help and nothing to do about it except try to breathe as she stared at his still chest, her thoughts arriving backward.

Population control…

Money and population control…

Intellecta invented the heart to get money and handle population control…

A hand shook her. "Jessica, we have to go!"

Detached, she looked slowly at Ayden's team gathering up the camera and gunning their motorcycles.

"Jessica!"

"What?" she snapped, her new reality fighting to infiltrate

her comfortable life.

"We have to *go!*"

Despite the urgency in pink-haired Hacker's voice, Jessica couldn't feel it herself. "Why?"

"Alarms tripped when we cut the power."

Jessica didn't know what that meant. But she *did* know they had to gather Ayden's body and take him to his parents who lived on level 1165, house number 811. She jumped to her feet. "We need to take his body back!"

A barking man's voice cut clear through the dark, and Jessica's heart skipped two beats before she realized Hacker carried a radio on her hip. "Three miles out," said a different voice from the radio.

Hacker grabbed Jessica's arm and yanked her toward her motorcycle. "Casualty of war," she shouted above the din of the two other roaring motorcycles. "Ayden knew we'd have to leave him. Since he was right about the Intella-heart's connection to population control, we have to assume Intellecta is listening to this same radio traffic, and go so far as to assume they have also tapped into the cameras surrounding this area. Which means they've already ID'd Ayden. Which means—"

"Shut up!" Jessica shrieked, sobbing. "I can use my imagination!"

Hacker didn't appear to be the kind of girl who cried. More like, drank the tears of the girls who did, because she sneered at Jessica alternating between weeping and screaming and wrangled her onto the back of her motorcycle. It shot forward so fast, Jessica nearly fell off the back.

She ducked her head and squeezed Hacker hard around her middle, the thump of Jessica's heart overcoming the roar of the motorcycles speeding down the ancient dark highway. They did not turn on their lights; careening through the darkness anyway. They were going to crash into something and Jessica was literally going to die. She didn't know how they could have the courage to drive that fast with nothing but starlight to light their way, have the courage to leave Ayden's body, to fight population control, defy Intellecta, risk their lives—

Lights far to their left approached from the sky, angling toward the skyscraper. Jessica watched the hovercopter touch down.

Sizzle on the motorcycle next to them shouted something. Jessica didn't hear, but Hacker looked sharply into the sky. She looked too, and once she saw the stars blotted out by a big, moving machine—driving straight at them—she picked out the whirling engines of a hovercopter. The hovercopter did not have its lights turned on.

Hacker slowed her motorcycle, the others following. Jessica didn't question it until Hacker removed her bag, spun on her seat, and thrust it at Jessica.

"What are you doing?" Sizzle asked.

"We have to hope that hovercopter is anyone but Intellecta," Hacker shouted for all of them to hear. "But in case it's not, we need to distract it while Jessica runs away with the camera. Jessica, there are several wireless pucks in the small front pocket. They will power on along with the city's power. They are set to link to the first available device automatically."

"M-me?" Jessica hiccuped, wiping her nose.

"As soon as the power comes back on, upload the video." "What are you—"

A merciless shove nearly toppled Jessica off the motorcycle. She twisted her body to adjust, just barely landing on her feet when Hacker shot forward on her motorcycle, flipping on her bright headlight, the other two close behind.

She watched a moment, stunned, scared, unsure, as the motorcycles shrunk in the distance without her. She wasn't a runner. Could not remember the last time she'd ran. High school? Propelling forward, she sprinted as if she'd been doing it every day for the past ten years, her feet somehow knowing how to *thump-thump-thump* in a rhythm to carry her away from a danger she did not trust even existed. Even so, she alternated between running away from the road toward a crumbling ground building and watching the distance shrink between hovercopter and motorcycle.

She stopped to catch her breath, pressing against a crumbling concrete wall. Similar structures spread the landscape all the way to the city where she could more easily disappear.

Disappear.

A moment of devastation slammed into her, hot and cold at the same time. She was in the video she had to upload. Intellecta would push out a "missing person" on her, complete with her hobbies, habits, and picture. She'd have to live on ground zero like Ayden!

She forced several, calming breaths. Maybe it wasn't like that at all. Maybe that hovercopter was the city's electrical team coming to turn the power back on. Maybe it was the police checking out the source of cut power. Maybe—

Brilliant gunfire spit out of the hovercopter in a shower of fire and death, raining upon the three motorcycles.

Jessica screamed.

The gunfire stopped. The hovercopter lowered to the ground in the rising cloud of smoke and fire it had birthed.

Jessica choked—heaved up her last meal—and screamed again. People jumped out of the hovercopter, flashlights shooting across the side of it. Even as far away as Jessica shook, she recognized the stylized "I" emblazoned on the side of the vehicle.

The same "I" she crossed under as she walked into work every day. The same "I" burned onto Ayden's chest.

Any lingering doubts she had about anyone being so wicked shriveled.

Sobbing, she ran, able to move at all because the survival portion of her brain fueled her limbs to get away from the danger while her mind throbbed with what she needed to do.

Needed to do.

She needed help.

Who would help her? She couldn't think. Couldn't reach out

to even the police until the WebNet came back with the power.

One foot in front of the other, breathing once in a while. That's all she could do. The city had disappeared in the dark, just a black mass somewhere in the distance. Then the lights flared on suddenly, momentarily disorienting her.

Her earcuff chimed on. Connected to the WebNet through the wireless puck in the bag.

Upload it as soon as the power comes back on.

She slipped her arms out of the straps on the bag, shaking so hard she couldn't pinch the zipper. She stopped, looked to where the men from the hovercopter walked around the wreckage they caused.

Maybe Intellecta wasn't tapped into the cameras at the skyscraper. Maybe they just had access to the radio. Maybe...maybe they don't know I'm involved.

She looked down at the bag the men from the hovercopter were probably looking for, looking for anything that would incriminate them. *Ten thousand people*, the news anchor said.

Jessica's comfortable job.

Ayden's last breath.

Her happy home she'd lived in for six years.

Childless parents on level 1165, house number 811.

Access to the WebNet which connected all her friends.

She sobbed into her knees, rocking back and forth. Back and forth. If she released that video, she was *literally* going to...no...*no*...she was *not. Going. To. Die!*

She forced her head up, forced herself to look again at the hovercopter spinning up to fly away, watch *Intellecta* fly away, after having murdered three people, after having installed a fatal heart in Ayden's chest. *Ten thousand people*, the news anchor said.

Jessica ripped open the bag and pulled the camera out, fumbling until she found the clearly marked "WebNet" switch and turned it on, accessing the camera's options to upload.

It took her just under a minute. During that eternity, the

wind cutting across the Salt Flats became the whirl of the hovercoptor, every blinking city light ahead of her, gunfire.

The camera finished uploading, and from there she sent a link to the news, and uploaded it to her own social and her huge following. Finished, she sat back against her hiding spot, closed her eyes, and listened through her earcuff to the shattering of her comfortable life.

...The heart saved your life, her own voice said. She knew what came next.

Those who chose to could replace their eyes with robotic ones. Those eyes could then be synced to their earcuff so they could watch the videos uploaded to their socials. Otherwise, all other people would be watching this video on monitors throughout the city, or at home.

*We did it...*Ayden's voice said. *Jessica, look...*

Jessica was neither in the city nor at home. Nor would she ever return if she hoped to live. She cried anew as word for word the video played in her ear, watching as Ayden died again. *Ayden!*

I was right.

Right about what?

...Population control...

The video finished.

In stunned silence, she barely blinked, only finally felt the chilling cold after several minutes with both butt and back pressed against the dirt and concrete.

"It's done, Ayden," she said, salted tears seeping through the corners of her mouth. "It's done."

Chapter Nine

"New message from Althea," her earcuff chimed like the robot it was, acknowledging neither humanity's moments of joy nor pain. *Althea?*

Clarity bit into her with rabid teeth.

"Earcuff, call Althea."

"Calling Althea."

Her sister picked up in two rings. "Jessica, I heard the power —" "Althea! Someone's out to kill me!"

A pause. "What happened?"

In horribly stressed, jumbled dialogue, Jessica told Althea everything, starting with her accidental trip to Understreet and ending with her crying as she hid in the shadows of Salt Lake, unable to enter, unable to walk away.

"The police will protect you," Althea said in a deadly serious tone. "Did you call them?"

"I don't know if Intellecta has hacked the network to my earcuff. They're the ones paying for it until the end of the week. If they have, and I tell they cops where to find me, Intellecta will get here first and kill me!"

"Why haven't they shut off your earcuff then since they know you were in the video?"

"Probably hoping I'll give away my location."

"What makes you think the cops aren't arresting Intellecta right now?"

"I don't know!" Jessica sobbed. "All I know is that I am safe for the moment without moving and with no one knowing where I am."

"I'm coming to get you."

"How will you know how to find me?"

"Keep listening to the news. If you hear that Intellecta has been arrested, it will be safer to give out your location. If not, we'll work it out when I get closer."

"Okay."

"Stay valiant now, you hear?"

"Okay."

Epilogue

Jessica sat on the couch, fingers clenched as she watched

the monitor with Althea, the news anchor delivering the news they'd been waiting an entire month for.

"On the twenty-fifth of September, Intellecta's CEO, Haverick Edelson, was accused of pre-planned mass execution with their own invention called the Intella-heart..."

Jessica's impatience had her wishing science would create something that would enable her to skim quickly through live feed to get to the only part she cared about.

After telling America about the damning video that first started the investigation into Intellecta's heart, the findings, and the hero-girl who courageously (Jessica sure didn't feel courageous hiding against a concrete wall balling her eyes out, wiping a drippy nose on her sleeve, as her known life crumbled at the conclusion of that video) exposed it all, the news anchor reported that Haverick Edelson, the CEO of Intellecta and a choice few others Jessica hardly knew, had all been found guilty of felonies according to the State of Utah.

Jessica and Althea both relaxed back into their chairs with a sigh. Jessica was finally safe. All the people who might have wanted to take their revenge out on her now faced execution. Charging someone with a felony was never taken lightly— thus the week-long investigation, even though Jessica wanted Haverick to face judge and jury the same night her sister picked her up at ground zero next to an RTP rail.

"Hero-girl..." Althea sipped her water, grinning.

"I don't want to be a hero. I'm just happy to feel safe again."

"Jephron thinks you're a hero." Jephron now worked at Loginetics in Las Vegas with her, he as a key member of their marketing team for their insertable BloodWise, and Jessica as their copywriter. "Especially since they wanted to implicate him for a felony, too, for marketing the heart, but you stuck yourself out there and defended him. I've never known you to be so bold!"

Well, once you've seen murder, run from murder, and saved ten thousand others from murder, you can't return to anything less, Jessica thought.

Althea said "bold" as if Jessica had been turned into a spice to throw on a dish to make it more robust; everything was now enhanced because of spicy Jessica. But, maybe life *was* a bit more enhanced because of her.

Jessica wasn't the only one who saw the stars a month ago. Once Jessica was sheltered away and safe from Intellecta's revenge, she dared to share her star experience with her social followers, initially thinking she was the only one who cared about them and wanted more. She was shocked to hear that her followers felt the same, and Jessica expressed how she *wished* the city lights would be shut down every once in a while just so everyone could see the stars. Suddenly thousands upon thousands of people were following her on her socials, holding her up so she could speak for them and petition Salt Lake City, Utah to shut off their lights just for an hour every month so they could see the stars.

Her wish was supported and voted upon. Salt Lake City agreed with Jessica, the ripple effect touching Las Vegas. And Elko, Nevada. Lawton, Oklahoma. Bennington, Idaho. Fort Leonard, Missouri. Ciudad Juarez, Mexico. And city after city until all of America agreed on a date and a time once a month to go dark.

Today it rained. But tonight, she would see Ayden's stars.

ABOUT THE AUTHOR

Virginia Parrish

Virginia Parrish is a graduate of Rutgers University and spent her childhood in the Philadelphia area. Since then, she has traveled widely and lived in various locations from Colorado to the UK to Texas. She has been writing since childhood and is currently working on a science-fiction trilogy set a couple of millennia in the future.

ABOUT THE AUTHOR

Andrew Bockhold

Andy Bockhold teaches high school English and Creative Writing in Cincinnati, Ohio, United States. His short fiction has appeared in Longreads, Bartleby Snopes (Pushcart Nominee), Streetlight Literary Magazine, and he has written film commentary for Taste of Cinema. He is also a contributing editor at Story Literary Magazine. Andrew's work and information can be found online at  andrewbockhold.com, @andrewbockhold on Twitter and @chewbockhold on Instagram.

ABOUT THE AUTHOR

Sammi Caramela

Sammi is a writer, fiction author, and poet. When she isn't putting pen to paper, she's spending time with loved ones, practicing yoga, reading on her balcony, or dancing to one of her carefully-curated playlists. Check out her mental health  and wellness blog/podcast (Sammi Says) or connect with her on Instagram @sammicaramela. Sammi loves to hear from her readers!

ABOUT THE AUTHOR

Ellen Parry Lewis

Ellen Parry Lewis is the author of seven young adult novels and one non-fiction book. She has also worked as an editor and author for other short story collections. Before making the switch to fiction, Ellen worked as a freelance reporter for several newspapers. She also currently works at her alma mater, Rowan University, teaching writing. Ellen lives in New Jersey with her husband, daughter, son, elderly dachshund, fluffy Labrador retriever, and atypically grumpy hamster.

Social Media:

Facebook: facebook.com/ellenparrylewis
Twitter: @ellenparrylewis
Insta: ellenparrylewis
Website: ellenparrylewis.com

ABOUT THE AUTHOR

David Sangiao-Parga

David Sangiao-Parga is a 40-year-old father of 4. He has a MFA from Florida International University and lives in Ft. Lauderdale, FL. His debut novel, "Blood In the Holler", will be released later this year from Woodhall Press.

ABOUT THE AUTHOR

J. M. Robison

Hello book worms! Unless you prefer book dragon? I am J.M. Robison. I write fantasy books where heroes don't follow the rules. FUN FACT: I joined the U.S. Army at 17 with the sole goal in mind to learn how to write battle scenes realistically and experience different cultures to add variety to my world building and characters (to date I have visited Italy, Germany, Romania, Bulgaria, Afghanistan, Qatar, U.A.E., and Kuwait.)

PERSONALITY: Introverts unite! Separately of course.

WHAT I LIKE: reading! Because you should never trust and author who does not also read. I crochet. I strive to be chemical-free so I make my own body and household products which are cheap and non-toxic (shampoo, laundry, soap, toothpaste, face cleaner, face moisturizer). I love mountain biking and camping. And video games! I'm on discord: Evermore#3394. Recently I started barefoot running...and I love it!

WHAT I WANT: Going to become a hermit when I retire. Like, legit live in the mountains hunting, gathering, and building lean-tos.

WEBSITE: jmrobison.com

BOOKS BY THIS AUTHOR

Night Light: Haunted Tales Of Terror

Night Light: Haunted Tales of Terror will keep you up at night with tales of creatures from deep underground coal mines in the the Appalachian Mountains, ghostly apparitions, mysterious prayer circles, a pact with the devil and blood curdling screams of the Jersey Devil haunting a couple in the middle of the night in the New Jersey Pine Barrens. Featuring new suspense and horror stories from Mid-Atlantic authors Ellen Parry Lewis, SF Varney, Charles Matthew, Virginia Parrish and Sammi Caramela.

Some Place Like Home

April is different, and not just in the quirky-girl-in-converse kinda way. She doesn't stress about college applications or prom dates like the other seniors in her class. Instead, she cycles obsessions and fear ranging from vomiting to being a bad person. For the most part, April can hide behind her glasses and distract herself with the murder mysteries she's always reading. But every so often, her obsessive-compulsive disorder becomes so debilitating that she can't help but give into her compulsions. So when a classmate goes missing, April feels it's her responsibility to find him-and won't rest until she does.

Horror On Holiday: 13 Tales Of Terror

Horror on Holiday: 13 Tales of Terror is a bakers dozen of illustrated chilling stories from the mind of Jolene Wightman. Each story is set during a different holiday proving once and for all that horror is a year round affair. Featuring spooky and ethereal illustrations by SF Varney. Filled with stories of aliens, frightful creatures, witches and ghostly apparitions, this book is perfect for reading by flashlight under the covers. Read if you dare!

An Unremarkable Girl

Krisanna Wether happily lived in a peaceful farming village until it was raided and her people were enslaved by a neighboring kingdom. She finds herself in a dangerous situation where she is mistaken for a traveling princess. While living under this false identity, Krisanna meets a handsome, kind enemy soldier who makes her question her hatred towards her captors. Her feelings toward him blossom, enveloping him in her dangerous web of deceit.

Because She Fell Asleep

Ember Amato is the prototypical high school senior, with a busy schedule, great friends, and a caring boyfriend. But her life takes a surprisingly dark turn when her best friend, Janell, falls asleep on the school bus one morning, waking up at a ramshackle house in the woods. Though presumably telling Ember all about the strange conversation she overheard there, Janell's disappearance one night speaks of her having held some information back. In pursuit of her best friend, Ember discovers a brutal murder. Fearing that a police investigation has grown cold, Ember puts it upon herself to look into these horrifying occurrences, However, in so doing, she sets off an unpredictable and dangerous chain of events.

How To Become A Valedictorian

Being the valedictorian or salutatorian of your graduating class may open many doors, including valuable scholarships to attend college and coveted high profile internships to help get a step ahead of your classmates. Becoming a valedictorian is hard work, but just getting straight A's may not be enough. In Smarty-Pants: How to Become a Valedictorian, Ellen Parry Lewis shares her personal story, along with stories from other valedictorians on the specific strategies and actions they took to earn the honor of being chosen as valedictorian for their graduating class.

Future Vision

Samantha Bell is an ambitious high school student with a bright future until one fateful night at the local fair. She decides to go through the controversial Future Vision exhibit. This attraction allows viewers to see up to twenty seconds of their personal future. Because of the possible risks, viewers must ingest a dissolvable pill immediately afterward, causing them to forget what they had just witnessed. Samantha tries to take the future into her own hands, though, when she smuggles a pen inside the attraction. Although she was forced to forget what she had seen, she leaves the attraction with an ominous feeling and three mysterious words written on her hand: Snow, fight, and ca. Samantha feels she must figure out what those three words mean before the event occurs and possibly ruins her life.

METAL LUNCHBOX PUBLISHING